For Mom & Dad—JSM and CS

PENGUIN WORKSHOP
An imprint of Penguin Random House LLC, New York

First published in the United States of America by Penguin Workshop,
an imprint of Penguin Random House LLC, New York, 2023

Text copyright © 2023 by James S. Murray and Carsen Smith
Illustrations copyright © 2023 by Penguin Random House LLC

Insert illustrations by Patrick Spaziante

Insert HUD assets: NatalyaBurova/iStock/Getty Images, Nattapon Kongbunmee/iStock/Getty
Images, PlargueDoctor/iStock/Getty Images, SerGRAY/iStock/Getty Images, St_Aurora72/
iStock/Getty Images, Veronika Oliinyk/iStock/Getty Images

Visit us online at penguinrandomhouse.com.

Library of Congress Cataloging-in-Publication Data is available.

Book manufactured in Canada.

ISBN 9780593226162   10 9 8 7 6 5 4 3 2 1 FRI

Design by Jay Emmanuel

AREA·51 INTERNS
TIME CHASERS

BY JAMES S. MURRAY
AND CARSEN SMITH

PENGUIN WORKSHOP

CHAPTER ONE

THIRTEEN YEARS AGO . . .

The arch of electricity curved over the top of the machine as the metal apparatus came to life, crackling and sizzling like a bug zapper.

Ernest Becker watched it through the glass window from the nearby observation room. He had waited for this moment his entire life, and so he tried to ignore the fact that the compression suit meant to monitor his vital signs was starting to itch. He wished he'd chosen a comfier outfit for traversing the space-time continuum.

But there was no turning back now.

A knock at the door pulled his attention away from the impressive electrical display.

Ernest felt his heart clench upon seeing it was Cassandra Harlow who had joined him in the small room. His mind swirled as he tried to sort out everything he wanted to say to her, but she took the decision out of his hands by speaking first.

"Are you sure about this?" Cassandra asked. Ernest could hear the tiniest shake to her voice.

"If everything goes according to plan, you won't even notice I'm gone." Ernest smiled. "You trust me, don't you?" He took her hand in his. Her eyes twinkled under the lights of the time machine.

"You're sure you don't want a team to go with you?" Cassandra pressed. "It's not too late to change your mind."

"I can't risk losing anybody else," Ernest said. "It's my machine. If anyone should go, it should be me."

Cassandra crossed her arms. An uneasiness filled the silent space between them.

"You want anything while I'm out?" Ernest asked with a raised brow. "Whatever you want. Cleopatra's necklace? Amelia Earhart's goggles? One of Queen Victoria's crowns?"

Cassandra smirked. "Leave it to you to make the first manned mission through time sound like you're going Christmas shopping."

"You're right. Who am I kidding? Guess I'll have to settle for a Super Bowl ring from 1978."

"Now that you mention it, I suppose I wouldn't mind one of Marie Curie's beakers."

"Say no more. I bet she won't even notice it's gone," Ernest said with a grin.

Cassandra sucked in a sharp breath and stepped back by the door. "Ernest . . . all I want is for you to get back in one piece."

"Cassandra . . . ," Ernest started. He turned toward the window, resting his gaze upon the time machine.

"Yeah?"

"I've been wanting to tell you something for a while now . . ." He trailed off again, his breath fogging up the glass.

"What is it, Ernest?" Cassandra asked.

Ernest bit the inside of his lip. Risking his life by traveling through time felt less scary than trying to get out the words that had been building up for so long.

Is now the right time? What if . . . I don't make it home?

No. I'll make it home. And we'll have the rest of our lives to figure this out.

"How about this? I promise to tell you when I get back," he said with a gentle smile. "And it will definitely be worth it."

Cassandra raised a curious eyebrow, but before she could respond, a buzz came from her hip. She glanced down at the message and then back up to Ernest.

"That's Director Martinez. He says it's time."

Cassandra opened the door and motioned toward the hall. Ernest took one last deep breath as their hands brushed against each other's on the threshold.

Stepping into the time machine bay, Ernest suddenly felt claustrophobic. A hundred faces looked back at his. A whole array of Area 51 employees had come to watch the historic occasion. Their expressions ranged from excited to petrified, a perfect amalgamation of Ernest's own feelings.

Slowly but surely, a wave of applause overtook the crowd. Ernest couldn't help but feel humbled by the outpouring of admiration from the nation's top scientific minds.

Director Martinez intercepted the two of them.

"Everything is set and ready to go; the same parameters as the last fifty test runs," Director Martinez said. "Now, don't you go forgetting about us during all of your incredible travels!"

Ernest ran a hand through his hair. "Oh, don't worry, Director Martinez. I could never forget about you."

The director gave a hearty chuckle and took his place at the control station. Ernest stepped into position in front of the large pod. His heart began to beat wildly against his temporal transporter device that hung against his chest. Much like his suit's itchiness, he questioned why he'd made the important time dial quite so heavy.

He peered around the back wall at the numerous time machine prototypes lined up in the bay. The first few were in shambles, shattered pieces of titanium that couldn't hold up against the powerful portals they created. The more recent prototypes had been successful in transporting androids, plant life, and even mice through time. Each represented one step closer to this moment—the moment when Ernest's life's work would finally all be worth it.

Director Martinez and the members of Ernest's Continuum Navigation team hovered over the control panel. In synchronicity, they revved up the power feeding to the center machine. All that was left was for Ernest to step inside, set his coordinates on the interior time machine dashboard, and let the portal do the rest.

The voltage swelled into the metallic dome. Electricity zapped faster and faster until the rhythm morphed into one continuous thrumming sound.

Ernest looked over his shoulder one last time. Cassandra mouthed the words he had been searching for all this time: *I love you.*

The doors closed behind him with a resounding clang.

He looked down at his temporal transporter and twisted the dial, aligning the clock on his chest to the coordinates set into the dashboard.

Within an instant, the time portal swirled to life inside the machine. It was even more beautiful than he ever could've imagined—a churning spiral of vivid colors and shimmering silver dust. Ernest felt his hands ball up into fists by his side. He steadied his nerves, stepped into the spinning mass of particles, and felt his own atoms disassemble as his body was thrust into the space-time continuum.

Cassandra held her breath, waiting for Ernest's safe return. All the oxygen in the room felt like it had been sucked out through the portal with him.

She blinked her eyes and squeezed them hard, hoping that when she opened them, Ernest would be standing there with his gleaming smile as brilliant as ever.

The question built up in her throat like a punch. "Shouldn't he be back by now?"

Director Martinez curled his fingers around his chin.

Steam drifted and swirled in the place where the time machine had been sitting. When the vapor finally cleared, there was nothing.

No Super Bowl ring.

No Marie Curie souvenirs.

No time machine.

No Ernest.

Alarms exploded from the control panel.

"What's happening?" Cassandra shouted. "What's wrong?"

Director Martinez and the rest of the Continuum Navigation team spread out across the control panel in a flurry of typing fingers and dizzying scrolling.

"His tracking signal . . . ," Director Martinez said. "It—it just disappeared!"

Cassandra pushed her way through to the control panel. "What about his vitals? Can we still get a read on those?"

She peered down at the blinking coordinates dancing in a chaotic whirl across the screen. The numbers showing Ernest's heart rate and blood pressure values fizzled out before her very eyes.

Director Martinez's typing slowed until eventually, his hands grew completely still.

"Cassandra . . . ," Director Martinez said. "We knew this was a possibility. Ernest knew the risk he was taking."

"No!" Cassandra cried. "There's got to be a way to get him back!"

Tears stung at her eyes as she fiddled with the trackpad, desperately trying to lock back onto Ernest's time signature. But it was no use. The calculations jumbled together on the space-time map. It was as if he'd disappeared from existence entirely.

She pushed her way through the crowd toward the row of time machines against the back wall. She slapped her palms against the metal doors of the prototype machine next to where Ernest's pod had stood moments ago.

"Let me in!" she shouted. "I'm going after him!"

Director Martinez pulled gently on her shoulders, trying to peel her away.

"I'm so sorry, Cassandra. There's nothing we can do now," Director Martinez said, shaking his head.

"He's lost."

CHAPTER TWO

PRESENT DAY . . .

Viv Harlow had only been an intern at Area 51 for a little over a week, and already the life she used to live—life as a normal twelve-year-old—felt like a distant memory.

Eight days ago, she and her best friends managed to rescue hundreds of Area 51 employees from an attempted alien abduction. Viv had taken that . . . well, not in stride, but it seemed easier to accept literal aliens than the scene that had just played out before her.

Viv stared down at the shards of broken glass glistening like a million stars by her feet. She rubbed at her eyes, hoping that what she'd just seen was all a bad dream. All the unicorns, mermaids, and werewolves she'd spent the whole night wrangling back into the Forbidden Zone were one thing. Just another day at Area 51. But seeing a man appear out of thin air, tell her that he was her long-lost father, and then vanish again was something Viv couldn't bring herself to believe.

After all, she had been awake since 3:00 a.m., and the possibility that her mind was playing tricks on her was an alluring thought.

This can't be happening. This can't be real!

But one look at her mom, and Viv knew she wasn't dreaming.

"Mom?" Viv said. "That man . . . you called him Ernest. That was Ernest Becker, wasn't it? The man from the old photograph?"

Her mother looked like she'd been turned to stone. The tray of vials Cassandra had dropped when the man appeared sat in a shattered heap on the ground. Viv swallowed down the lump in her throat.

"He said he was my dad," Viv said. "Is that true?"

Still no answer.

"Mom? Mom?!" Her frustration grew by the second. "Mom, answer me!"

Finally, Cassandra's eyes blinked in rapid succession, and she took a deep breath.

"Follow me."

Her mom swept the shattered glass on the ground across the floor with her heel, gripped Viv's wrist, and yanked her daughter down the corridor.

"Mom?!" Viv said. "What's going on? Please! Talk to me!"

They made it a few steps before Viv managed to wrestle her arm away.

"Mom, stop!" Viv said. "Enough secrets!"

Her mother turned to her with tears in her eyes. A tiny smile broke through as she spoke. "You trust me, don't you, Viv?"

The question made Viv's head pound. So much had happened in the past week; so many secrets had come to light that made Viv wonder if she even knew her mother at all.

Viv's entire world had flipped upside down when the horde of Roswellian aliens had escaped, and it turned out that her mom's "boring office job" at Area 51 was anything but boring. It was during that invasion when Viv had found out she had been born with alien DNA . . . and hidden alien powers. But the truly earth-shattering part was that it was her mom's experimentation with alien DNA while unknowingly pregnant that gave Viv her powers in the first place. And even worse, her mom had no idea what she had done to her own daughter.

Viv had tried so hard to force her powers down where no one could ever see them. How could she trust her mom to accept her after everything Cassandra had done? But ultimately it hadn't mattered. Last night, while corralling hundreds of dangerous creatures running rampant through the halls of Area 51, Viv had been forced to use her powers in public. She and her friends had managed to save the day again . . . but not without Viv's worst fear coming true: her mom finding out about her alien abilities.

Sure, her mom seemed to be supportive, offering to help run some tests to "figure this out." But did that mean figuring out how to help control her powers for Viv's benefit or because her mom was scared of Viv's abilities? They hadn't even had the chance to take her pulse before they were interrupted by Ernest Becker's appearance.

Which brought Viv to the real reason she wasn't sure if she could trust her mom: For Viv's entire life, no matter how hard she tried, she could never get her mom to reveal anything about her father. Not his name, what he did for a living. Not even whether he was alive or dead.

So Viv stood completely still.

Her mother sighed. "Whether you trust me or not, we don't have much time. I promise, I'll explain everything soon. But right now, we need to move."

Viv tried to protest, but the fatigue made it tough. They hustled around corner after corner, whizzing by the other employees arriving for the day. Instead of the normal hellos and good mornings, Viv's mom kept her head down—a woman on a mission. After a few minutes, the two arrived at a large steel door cordoned off with caution tape.

Viv watched as her mom pressed her palm into the scanner. The familiar voice of Area 51's automated security system spilled out into the hallway.

"Identity confirmed: Director Cassandra Harlow. ACCESS DENIED."

"Denied? You've got to be kidding me," Viv's mom said.

She punched a long numerical code into the door, but the message was still the same.

"ACCESS DENIED."

"Back up," Cassandra said, reaching into her interior blazer pocket.

Viv shuffled a few paces and watched as her mom pulled out her plasma pistol. She shot straight at the door.

ZAP!

The blast blew a hole right through the door's latching device, melting the metal and the caution tape like an ice sculpture on a hot Nevada day.

"MOM?!" Viv shouted. "What are you doing?!"

Sirens wailed from inside the sealed-off room.

"Come on, Viv," Cassandra said. "We've gotta keep moving."

Her mom reached in and disabled the alarm system. She pushed the doors open manually and pulled Viv inside before flipping on the lights.

In comparison to the rest of the Area 51 compound, this room looked . . . old. Instead of touchscreens and holograms, everything was controlled by buttons and dials. There was even more dust in here than there was in the old filing room.

Whoa. What is this place?

Cassandra punched a few digits into her high-tech watch.

"Desmond? Sabrina? I need you to come back to the base

right away. It's an emergency," Cassandra said into the watch, "Call Nicolás and Al, too. Meet me in the old Continuum Navigation wing. I'll explain everything once you get here."

Viv hoped that her friends' parents would bring them along, too. Viv had faced down aliens, cryptids, even dinosaurs with Charlotte, Elijah, and Ray at her side. But she needed them now more than ever.

Hold on a second . . . Continuum Navigation?

Viv examined the room more closely. On the back wall, a lineup of strange, dilapidated machines of various sizes sat in a row, each larger and more complex than the last. Wires and plugs fed into them all like some kind of mad scientist's experiments, and cobwebs had proliferated into every corner of the room. The entire place gave Viv the heebie-jeebies.

"Mom?" Viv said. "Where are we?"

"An abandoned section of the base," she explained. "The director before me, Director Martinez, closed it down over a decade ago. He deemed it too dangerous for any further experiments after—"

"After what?"

"After . . . Ernest Becker went missing."

Viv felt the hairs on the back of her neck stand up.

"Went missing?" Viv said. "What do you mean? But we just saw him? Went missing where?"

"Went missing . . . in time."

In time?

The machines against the wall . . . the *Continuum Navigation* wing . . . the way Ernest Becker was flickering in and out . . . The pieces finally fell into place in Viv's mind.

"Those are time machines, aren't they?"

Cassandra pulled a plastic sheet off a large table near the middle of the room.

"If I can just get this system up and running, it should be exactly how we left it . . ."

In one swift motion, Viv's mom assembled an array of plugs, flipped the switches on the fuse box, and brought the machines to life.

"Yes! Now, since I know he was at this moment in time"—she glanced down at her watch—"exactly sixteen minutes and twelve seconds ago, using that, plus the coordinates of his initial launch, I should be able to pinpoint his location."

Cassandra typed a myriad of numbers into the retro screen's display and pressed Enter. The locator icon spun around in a huge elliptical loop.

Finally, a ring of points lit up on the map like a Christmas tree.

"There you are," Cassandra said. "I've got you now."

A voice from the back of the room nearly startled them both out of their pants.

"Director Harlow?"

It was Al Mond, Ray's dad. Behind him, his son cradled Meekee, his tiny alien best friend, in his arms. Charlotte Frank and her parents entered carefully, avoiding the melted patch in the door. Elijah Padilla and his dad stepped in just a few paces behind.

"Thank goodness you all got here so quickly," Cassandra said.

"We'd barely left the parking lot," Lieutenant Nicolás Padilla said. "What the heck happened to the door?"

"The door isn't important right now. But what is important is that . . . Ernest is alive, and he was just on the base," Cassandra replied.

A shockwave of gasps rippled on the faces of every parent in the room.

"What?! Are you kid—" Desmond Frank said before being cut off.

"Al, I need you to take the kids to the observation room and hold them there. Don't let them out of your sight," Director Harlow said, motioning toward a side door against the left wall of the room.

Without a second of doubt, Mr. Mond snapped to attention, draping his arm over Ray's and Viv's shoulders.

"Let's go, kids. You heard the boss," Mr. Mond said.

"Wait!" Viv said. "Let us help!"

"I'm sorry, sweetie," Director Harlow said. "This is far too dangerous."

Cassandra turned her attention to the remaining parents.

"The rest of you—I want you here manning the controls."

Mr. Mond motioned toward his left.

"Manning the controls for what?" Viv asked. "Please, we can help!"

"Vivian, enough! I don't have time to argue with you; I need to you go with Mr. Mond," her mom said. "Now!"

Viv recoiled. She knew her mom had a reputation of being demanding with her employees at work, but Viv had never heard her snap like that.

Especially not directed at me . . .

Mr. Mond opened the door to the small observation room and shuffled the four kids inside. Viv wanted to fight back, to stay by her mom's side no matter what, but one look at the steely look in her eyes and she knew there was no changing her mother's mind.

The door closed behind them with a heavy clack, leaving Viv feeling utterly useless.

❋❋❋❋❋

Director Harlow turned back to face her team, the most trusted group of scientists and engineers Area 51 had to offer. Desmond, Sabrina, and Nicolás looked back at her with curious expressions and crossed arms.

"Ernest is alive, and I'm going after him," Cassandra said.

Desmond ruffled the back of his hair. Nicolás shifted his weight.

"I say this with all due respect, but are you out of your mind?" Sabrina said. "We were all there that day. You heard what Director Martinez said. I'm sorry, but he's gone, Cassandra."

"Look at this," Director Harlow said, brushing even more dust off the screen. "See this ellipse here? It's Ernest's signal."

"What? How did you possibly pick that up?" Desmond said.

"He was here. In the base. He showed up right after you all left."

Desmond and Sabrina swapped uncertain looks.

"We always assumed the problem must be with his temporal transporter," Cassandra said. "It's supposed to allow us to track him even while it allows his atoms to disassemble and reassemble within the time machine's time portals. We've never been able to latch back onto his signal, so we all reasoned that the device must have malfunctioned after his first jump."

"Right," Desmond said. "Because we were never able to track his coordinates."

"Exactly. But now that I have an exact time location point from when he just appeared, I was able to lock back onto his time signature and pull up his coordinates," Cassandra continued. "We couldn't trace his temporal transporter back then because he's been circling the same points in time over and over again too fast to pick up on his signal!"

"Cassandra . . . ," Sabrina said. "That's a good theory, but he's been gone well over a decade. How can you be sur—"

"I know what I saw," she said. "He's alive. Viv saw him, too."

She wrote furiously on the whiteboard, calculating the arc of Ernest's coordinates.

"Now that we have an exact time and location for him, I can use that to lock onto his time signature and start following him through time to try to catch up to him!"

Desmond placed a gentle hand on Cassandra's shoulder.

"I'm not even sure those machines still work, Director," Desmond said.

"We don't have time to run any tests. According to my initial calculations, the strength of his time signature will downgrade exponentially if we don't follow it within an hour of his appearance in person. And then it'll be too late to lock onto his signal and his points in time. This might be my only chance to get him back," Cassandra said. "I need to know if you're all with me or not."

Sabrina, Desmond, and Nicolás let out a collective breath. They didn't look happy, yet slowly but surely, they all nodded in agreement.

"Then it's decided," Cassandra said. "I need you all here tracking my coordinates and my vitals."

"At least let one of us go with you, in case whatever happened to Ernest happens again," Desmond said.

"Under no circumstances are any of you to enter those time machines. Is that clear?" Cassandra's voice was like ice.

"He was our friend, too. We could help track him down," Nicolás chimed in.

"He *is* your friend. He's not dead yet," Cassandra said. "You can help from here."

"But what happens if you're lost, too?" Sabrina asked. "What will happen to Viv?"

Cassandra steeled her nerves and wiped a drop of sweat away from her forehead. That particular version of failure had only crossed her mind briefly, but now that someone else was suggesting the possibility, it suddenly felt like a plausible outcome.

No. No, I can do it. I'll figure it out. I could never leave Viv all alone.

"If Ernest can find a way to make it back, then so can I."

CHAPTER THREE

Viv stared through the glass from the observation room. On the walls behind her, rows of closets and drawers secured with heavy bolt locks loomed tall overhead. The entire room had a stale, mildewy smell to it, like a locker room that hadn't been cleaned in years.

She watched her mom in the Continuum Navigation wing gesturing and typing into the control panel with Charlotte's parents and Elijah's dad crowded around her.

"Viv?" Elijah said with a yawn. "Do you have any idea what's going on?"

"Yeah, why the heck did they call us back in? I was excited to get some sleep," Ray said. "See? I already put Meekee in his pajamas."

The mango-size alien snoozing on Ray's shoulder was squeezed into a homemade, threadbare set of race car jammies, custom fit with four leg holes.

Viv lowered her voice down to a whisper, hoping that Mr.

Mond was too focused on the other parents to hear them.

"Hey, guys . . . ," Viv said. "Remember that picture of our parents we found in the file room?"

Charlotte joined in on the huddle. "Yeah? The one when they were all young?"

"That man in the photo . . . ," Viv said. "Ernest Becker? Well . . . I think he's my dad, and I think he's a time traveler."

Elijah's eyes opened as wide as two dinner plates. Ray's jaw practically hit the floor. Charlotte couldn't help but let out a snort.

"What, Charlotte?" Viv asked. "You don't believe me?"

"You know what," Charlotte said. "At this point, after everything I've seen here at Area 51, if you told me that your dad was a gummy bear with wings who spoke fluent Italian, I'd believe it."

"I think he's been lost in the space-time continuum, but he just came back for a second, and he said he was my dad, but now I think my mom might be trying to track him down so she's jumping into one of those time machines to find him, but she might get lost the same way that he did and—"

"Hold on, Viv. Slow down," Elijah said. "Those things out there . . . Those are time machines?"

"What? No way!" Ray shouted. "I thought they were big old Keurigs."

"Shh!" Viv said, grabbing Ray's collar as he tried to jerk toward the window to take a closer look. "Keep your voice down."

Viv looked over her shoulder and peered through the glass at her mom, still darting around the room.

"I can't believe Mom didn't tell me about any of this, not even after I learned the truth about her job . . . ," Viv said. "And now, she won't even let me go with her to find him!"

Elijah looked around at each face in the huddle. "Then what are we waiting around here for?" Elijah said.

"What do you mean?" Viv asked.

"If my dad was lost in the space-time continuum, and we were standing in front of the world's only time machines, I feel like the answer would be pretty clear."

Did he really just say what I think he said?

"You guys would travel through time for me? Even though it's super dangerous?"

"Of course!" Elijah said.

"Yeah, duh," Charlotte agreed. "You'd do the same for us."

"Are you kidding? I've always wanted to time travel!" Ray said. "I'm not doing this for you! I'd be doing this for me!"

Viv couldn't help the smile that spread across her face. Her friends had once again proven they were the best people on planet Earth.

But the smile faded as quickly as it came, as she felt a twinge of guilt shoot through her. How could she be asking Elijah and Ray to risk their lives for her and Ernest when she still hadn't told them the truth about her powers?

Last night, when Viv's powers had burst out of her to hold

back the cryptids, Joanna Kim had claimed her robotic ferret, FuRo, was the source of the energy. Viv had been grateful, although this favor wasn't quite enough to make up for Joanna's misguided decision to let all the creatures loose in the first place. If it were up to her, the boys would never find out her secret. It was already too much that her mom and Charlotte had found out themselves. The idea of Ray, and particularly Elijah, learning the truth and treating her like a freak was too scary to imagine.

"Okay, but how do we get past Ray's dad?" Charlotte asked.

The four kids all glanced over their shoulders at Mr. Mond, planted face-first against the observation window.

"Doesn't seem like it'll be too hard," Elijah said.

A knock at the door sent Mr. Mond and the kids scrambling backward. The latch clicked and in walked Viv's mom, straight-faced and moving briskly. Without a word, she hustled straight toward the back wall and opened one of the tall closets, digging through old boxes and plastic bins until she finally pulled out the strange device she'd been looking for.

It almost looked like an old-school alarm clock attached to a looped chain. She flicked the device on and situated it around her neck.

"Viv," her mom said, "I don't have a lot of time. But I want to tell you what's going on." She knelt, making sure their eyes were level, before she continued. "Remember when you asked me if Ernest Becker was your father, and I said he was a very good friend?"

Viv nodded. Was her mom finally going to be honest with her? She held her breath as the response came.

"The truth is . . . he *is* your father."

Ray let out an audible gasp, forceful enough to wake Meekee from his slumber.

Viv felt her heart clench in her chest.

I was right. He's alive.

I knew it.

"Why didn't you tell me about him before?" Viv asked. "You had thirteen years, and you never thought to talk about him? Not once?"

"I didn't know what to say," Cassandra said. "I didn't know if he was alive or dead."

"You knew that he disappeared in a time machine!" Viv cried. "Don't you think I would've liked to know that?"

"I didn't want to tell you something that wasn't true," her mom explained. "He just disappeared, and we had no idea what had happened to him. If he was somehow still alive after all these years, I didn't want you to go through any unnecessary grief, mourning a dad you never knew. And if he was dead, I didn't want to give you any false hope that he might be coming back."

Viv understood, but she didn't want to. Every ounce of

her wanted to flip out, to kick and scream. And finally . . . she did.

"You should've told me!" Viv shouted, her voice cracking sharply. "You've kept EVERYTHING a secret! Your job! My dad! No matter how many times I asked, you wouldn't tell me anything!"

Viv could feel the beginnings of her power bubbling to the surface. Everything this past week had been building up, and she couldn't keep it in anymore. She felt like a bundle of TNT whose flame had finally reached the end of its wick.

Ray took a feeble step backward, alarmed by Viv's sudden outburst. Viv hated how he looked almost scared of her, even as she felt the heat behind her eyes continuing to rise.

No, not now! I can't let them see my powers!

Out of nowhere, Cassandra knelt and gave Viv a kiss on the cheek. The unexpected and tender contact worked. It was just enough of a distraction to melt Viv's burgeoning powers away.

Viv collected herself and took a deep breath.

"I've grown up my whole life not knowing anything about my dad," she said softly.

"That's why I'm doing this, baby," her mom said. "That's why I'm going to get him back. For you. For us both. But I need to go before we lose him again."

"You're going into one of the machines? Now?!"

"I love you, Viv," her mom said. "Stay here with your

friends. I promise, I'll be back soon."

"No! What if what happened to . . . Ernest happens to you, too?" Viv said. It still felt a little weird to call him "Dad."

"Please don't go! At least take me with you!" she offered.

"It's too dangerous," her mother said. "I have to go."

She leaned in close and whispered into Viv's ear. "As soon as I'm back, we're going to figure out your powers together. But until then, maybe you should keep them hidden. I don't want you to get hurt using them until we understand them better."

Viv was left speechless. She had to clench her fists to keep the waterworks at bay.

She thinks I'm a monster. An uncontrollable monster.

With a tight hug and a quick swipe of her wet eyes, Director Harlow turned on her heels and marched out the door back to the Continuum Navigation wing.

Viv tried to chase after her mom, but Mr. Mond quickly stepped in the way.

"I know it's tough, Viv, but you need to listen to your mother," he said, closing the door behind Director Harlow.

"No!" Viv shouted. She ran over to the window and watched as her mom made her way to the central machine. Viv banged on the glass.

"Mom!" Viv said. "Please!"

But she was too late. The electricity flowing from the connected ceiling wires began to flow into the machine. Viv shielded her face as the crackling and zapping nearly blinded everyone in the room. She squinted through the bright light and watched as her mother stepped into the open doors of the time machine. Her mom reached down, spun the dials on her alarm clock–like necklace, and with one last wave goodbye, the doors closed behind her.

At the control panel, Dr. Frank pushed up the final lever. Light, drenched in every color of the rainbow, exploded out of the time machine. The device steamed and sizzled like a barbecue grill before a bright flash obscured Viv's vision.

She shielded her eyes with her forearm as a tear rolled down her cheek. By the time the vapor had finally cleared the window, her mother . . . was gone.

CHAPTER FOUR

Viv pushed her way past Mr. Mond and rushed through the door into the Continuum Navigation wing.

"Wait! Stop!" Mr. Mond called out.

Charlotte, Elijah, and Ray were quick to follow. The steam from the vanished machine was still slowly dissipating throughout the room, and Viv managed to run up behind the control panel just in time to hear the Franks' frantic discussion.

"Do we still have a reading on her?" Dr. Frank asked.

Her husband scrolled through the space map until he managed to lock onto a single green point shining with light.

"Yes . . . no . . . This is strange. I'm still getting a weak signal from her temporal transporter. But then, look, there— that's the last coordinate we have for her, and the coordinate itself doesn't make any sense. It's much longer than any of the others, and it looks like it must have gotten scrambled."

Mr. Frank sighed. "Wherever she is, it seems like she's

stuck there. Something must have happened, but I don't know what."

Dr. Frank hung her head low as a silence fell over the room. Viv's heart thrummed loudly in her chest.

"What have we done?" Lieutenant Padilla whispered.

"We did what she asked us to do!" Dr. Frank said.

Viv scanned the old screen, taking in the huge, mapped grid of both geographical and chronological coordinates.

"Where'd you send her first?" Viv asked. "Before she got stuck?"

Her voice sent a jump through the three adults hovering over the control panel. They exchanged a furrowed glance.

"Viv? You shouldn't be in here," Mr. Frank said.

"Tell her, Desmond," Charlotte's mom said. "She has the right to know."

Mr. Frank sighed and nodded. He scrolled down through the grid until the cursor was right over a glowing green loop.

"From Ernest's time signature, we were able to track his signal to what seemed like a coordinate close to his stop here in the present, in 1978," Mr. Frank explained. "We sent your mom to the same time frame, precisely at the same coordinates.

"She should have found him here," he said, tapping on one point of the glowing loop. "But instead, we're picking up her time signature from all of these points. Seems like she's hopping around through different eras just like Ernest is.

"But look." He dragged his finger along the spiral map. "Their loops are off."

"How can that be?" Elijah's dad asked. "We calculated directly from Ernest's time signature."

"Maybe she found him, and they decided to do some sightseeing?" Ray offered.

Yet again, the sound of an extra voice sent a jolt through the already on-edge adults. Ray, Elijah, Charlotte, and Mr. Mond had joined in the semicircle.

"No way," Viv said. "Mom told me herself. She was going to get him back, and they'd both come home. Something must be wrong."

Dr. Frank shifted into position over the control panel and took a cursory glance over the map.

"Viv's right. Something is wrong," Dr. Frank said. She pulled up the massive screen of theorized coordinates.

"It looks like they were incredibly close," Dr. Frank says. "Only about an hour off from each other. But I wonder why Ernest keeps jumping in the first place . . ."

While the parents argued, Viv stared at the two green loops on the screen, ever so slightly off from each other.

An hour? Why would they be off by an hour?

Then all at once, it hit her.

"What about daylight saving time?" Viv asked.

"Daylight saving time? Of course, we calculated for that," Lieutenant Padilla said.

"Right, but daylight saving time only came into effect in the United States in 1918. And in other countries, some have never even used it," Viv said. "Meaning that depending on what specific point in space and time you're trying to get her to, you'll need to know that country's policies and when they started using daylight saving time. Even if you were traveling to a country that was following it, it would still affect all the time calculations—that must be why their loops are just slightly off!"

Dr. Frank moved toward the whiteboard, reexamining all the possible formulas from Director Harlow's detailed calculations. Instantly, Viv recognized her mom's handwriting.

"She's right," Dr. Frank said, dumbfounded. "How could we have missed that?"

"Everything happened so fast," Mr. Frank said. "She insisted on jumping in there immediately! There was no time to think!"

The three of them motioned to individual points along the loop tracking Cassandra Harlow's position.

"See this?" Dr. Frank said. "These dozen points are all before 1918."

"But look. They have her landing in Chile and Germany. Anybody know when they began observing daylight saving time?" Lieutenant Padilla said.

"How am I supposed to know the daylight saving time policies of Chile?" Mr. Frank replied.

"Hold on. Just give me a minute . . . ," Dr. Frank said. She rummaged through the old desk and whipped out some of the most ancient technology Viv had ever seen at Area 51—a piece of paper and a pencil.

Using the lists of both Ernest's and Cassandra's coordinates, Charlotte's mom worked out an algorithm in under sixty seconds. "Here," she said. "What about this? I solved for a coefficient that, when plugged into the larger equations, aligns their coordinate values. It should course correct for the daylight saving time issue."

Mr. Frank reviewed the scrawled piece of paper. "Are you sure it's going to work?"

"I'm not one hundred percent certain," Dr. Frank admitted. "I'm good at math, but chronomathematics is an entirely different field."

"Is there anyone we can call? Who at the base would have knowledge about this kind of thing?" Lieutenant Padilla asked.

"No one that I can think of. Director Martinez closed down this sector over a decade ago," Mr. Frank said. "We haven't had a chronometrist working at Area 51 since Ernest Becker himself. With Ernest jumping around in a loop, and Cassandra stuck at this indecipherable coordinate, we're gonna need one if we want to make sure this equation is correct."

A tap on her shoulder made Viv spin around. It was Elijah.

With a finger held up to his lips, he pointed toward the time machines, currently unguarded as the parents argued by the whiteboard.

"If we're gonna go, we should go now," Elijah whispered.

Viv considered it for a moment.

My mom's lost. Ernest . . . my dad's lost. There's no one else to go after them. What other choice do I have?

Viv looked into Elijah's eyes and nodded.

"Any idea how to get the time machine working?" Ray asked.

"I watched Dr. Frank from the observation room when she sent my mom," Viv said. "It's that lever right there."

Viv pointed at the control panel where the lever was pulled back into its original position.

"And I think we're gonna need these," Charlotte said.

She held out her arm. Strung around her wrist were four of the alarm clock–like necklaces. She passed them out in the huddle.

"Where'd you get those?" Ray asked. "And what are they?"

"I dunno. I stole 'em outta one of the lockers back there," Charlotte said. "But your mom was wearing one when she went in."

Viv put it around her neck. The whole thing felt bulky and strange. The current time ticked away on the large green digits.

"It's a temporal transporter," Viv said, tapping at the screen.

"A what?" Elijah asked.

"That's what Mr. Frank called it," Viv said. "I think this is how they track people through time."

"Then these will be good to have. Ya know . . . in case we get lost, too . . . ," Ray said sheepishly, placing his temporal transporter around his neck.

Viv stopped for a moment. She'd never considered that possibility before. Her friends, yet again, were risking their lives for her.

But not just for her. For her dad. Her smart, time travel–inventing dad.

Viv had always daydreamed about what her father was like, making up details about him she could pretend were true. But this—this was real. Each new piece of information about him felt precious, even the scary details, like him being lost in time. She wanted more of these real moments and details about him.

We have to bring him back.

"Meekee," Viv said. "Think you can use your powers to bring me that sheet of paper and pull that lever over there?"

"Meekee!" The little alien jumped up and down with approval, nearly ripping his pajamas.

"Okay, we gotta move. We'll go find my dad first, and then he can help us figure out where my mom is." Viv led the way.

One by one, the four kids sneaked around the control panel and toward the last remaining time machine that looked somewhat functional.

The four squeezed in and huddled together. The inside of the time machine was a technical marvel, a massive departure from the somewhat simplistic designs of the Continuum Navigation wing.

Mr. Frank noticed them first. "Kids? What are you doing in there?!"

"Go! Go!" Elijah said.

Viv looked around the dashboard of the time machine. There were hundreds of keys, switches, and buttons.

"Meekee, the paper!" Viv shouted.

Meekee glowed with a faint aura of green. The sheet of paper began floating through the air until it drifted right into Viv's hand.

"KIDS! Get out of there this instant!" Dr. Frank said.

The adults pushed past the whiteboard and scrambled toward the time machine.

"Close the door! Quickly!" Charlotte said.

Viv grabbed at a knob by the door and twisted. The steel doors slammed shut with a clang. A flurry of fists banged against it.

"Oh, you are so grounded, young lady!" Mr. Frank's muffled voice came through the door.

"What do we do?!" Ray yelled.

"Both my parents' coordinates are still logged in!" Viv said. "I just need to make sure the new algorithm is put in . . ."

She hesitantly keyed in the equation using a dial until, eventually, Dr. Frank's full algorithm appeared on-screen.

"Did you do it?" Charlotte said.

"I think?" Viv replied, looking down at the confusing dashboard.

"Then let's go!" Elijah said.

"Wait!" Viv said. "Fix the numbers on our necklace thingies! I think they have to match where we wanna go. That's what Mom did!"

Her friends did as instructed. There was only one thing left to do.

"Meekee! The lever!" Viv shouted.

Meekee glowed again. They couldn't see the lever from the inside of the time machine, but it must've worked. A burst of electricity zapped through the ceiling of the machine.

"Elijah! So help me if you—" Lieutenant Padilla said.

"Everybody hold on!" Charlotte said.

"To what?!" Ray asked.

Viv felt Elijah grab her hand and squeeze tight. The portal erupted open behind them, stretching from the floor of the time machine all the way to the ceiling; a swirling vortex of brisk blues and royal purples filled the air.

Elijah's face started to stretch and pull like a fun house mirror at the county fair as the portal drew him in.

Charlotte was next. Viv watched as her body spun and contorted until it vanished. Ray cried out as the portal sucked him in, too. He looked like a rubber ducky being swept down a bathtub drain. Viv felt the pull, like a powerful magnet, yanking at her very atoms and stretching her body like saltwater taffy.

Then everything went dark.

CHAPTER FIVE

Every part of Viv's body felt like she'd been thrown into a blender, as if someone had tried to make a Viv-flavored smoothie. The molecules in her head felt jumbled up, and she could still sense the swirling from the time portal even after her vision came back.

She and her friends ended up in a dizzy heap, piled on top of one another on the floor of the time machine.

"Crikey!" Charlotte said, clutching at her head. "Everyone still have their own teeth?"

The friends were slow to get up. Somehow, Ray had ended up at the bottom of the pile.

"I think I'm gonna puke," Ray said. "Or fart. Either way, get off me!"

Viv dusted herself off. Besides the low hiss of steam gathered at the ceiling, the inside of the time machine was eerily quiet.

"Did it . . . work?" Charlotte asked.

"If the calculations are correct . . . " Viv said, looking over the dashboard. She pulled on the lever by the door, and the steel slats slid open, revealing a most magnificent sight.

"We should be in 1978," Viv said with a smile.

A huge metropolis sprawled out in front of their eyes. The streets were crowded with more people than Viv had ever seen in her life, zigzagging in every which direction. Tall buildings nearly blocked out the sun, and the sound of disco music flowed from each open window. Vintage cars raced down the street, honking and sputtering at every turn.

"Whoa," Elijah said. "It totally worked! We're in the groovy '70s!"

"Seriously, guys. I don't feel too good," Ray said, clutching his gut. He looked as green as Meekee while he hunched over onto the sidewalk, crawling on his hands and knees. A few belches escaped from his mouth as he continued to speak. "I don't know why, but I expected time traveling to be more—"

The contents of Ray's stomach shot out of his mouth like a rocket, completely covering the sidewalk in front of him. He staggered back a bit, took a deep breath, and dabbed at the corner of his mouth with the neck of his shirt. "Comfortable?"

"Aw geez! Way to pull a Ray!" Charlotte said.

A fashionable couple walking by, dressed in bell-bottom pants and tie-dye tops, skipped over the puddle of puke. The woman giggled as the pair continued down the street.

"Where are we?" Elijah asked.

"It's New York City!" Viv said.

"No way!" Ray said in between burps. "We gotta go to Broadway. I'm dying to see *Wicked*!"

"I don't think it's out yet, genius," Charlotte said.

Viv watched as a group of hippies in ponchos examined their long beards in the reflection of a building's window. A woman standing next to them flashed a peace sign their way. She winked at the hippies, sending a laugh through the entire group.

"Everyone looks so happy," Elijah said.

Ray leaned over and whispered into Viv's ear. ". . . Should we tell them about the internet?"

Viv rolled her eyes. "Of course not! We shouldn't interfere with anything unless we have to. Try not to leave any trace that we were even here."

"Well, what about Ray's pile of puke on the sidewalk?" Charlotte pointed out.

Just as they all looked over their shoulders, another man walking by puked right on top of the pile of hurl Ray had left before stumbling away.

"Huh. Problem solved!" Ray said.

"Wow. New York in the '70s is a nonstop party, huh?" Elijah said.

Viv looked across the street, noticing a loud, bustling building where people flowed in and out.

A chalkboard sign out on the sidewalk in front of the club caught Viv's attention.

No way. It can't be.

"Hey, guys?" she said. "Do you see that place over there?"

The building seemed to be the epicenter of the social life. People funneled in like a massive house party.

"Is that a bar?" Ray asked.

"No, not a bar," Viv said. "It's a disco club!"

"Meekee dancey!" the little alien pipped from the inside of Ray's pocket.

"No, Meekee. No dancing today, buddy," Ray said, pushing him back down out of sight. "If these people don't know about the internet, I don't think they'll understand a little alien."

"Do you guys see that? Look at the sign!" Viv grabbed onto Charlotte's hand, and the friends wove their way through the crowd. The men were dressed in fine leisure suits and page boy hats. The women all wore their hair natural and looked bright, wearing an array of vibrant colors and patterns. Everyone gave odd looks at the comparatively blandly dressed children as they crossed the street.

Listed in calligraphy-style chalk handwriting, a list of various beverages ran down the length of the sign.

Mint Julep . . . Bloody Mary . . . and . . .

"The Ernest?" Elijah read aloud.

"That can't be a coincidence," Viv said. "Let's try to get in. I bet somebody in there knows how we can find my dad!"

Before they could react, the hefty door to the disco club swung open again. It was a man dressed in a flowery blouse, funky plaid pants, and sporting a thick mustache. He tossed a towel over the crook of his elbow and leaned up against the wall, lighting the grossest cigarette Viv had ever smelled in her life.

"Excuse me, sir?" Viv said.

"Four tickets to the disco club, please!" Ray said.

"Hi there. Please ignore my friend," Viv continued. "We're looking for my dad. Any chance you've seen him?"

"A lot of people have parents in there, little flower child," the man said, examining her strange apparel. "What's with the square threads?"

He pointed at the temporal transporter hanging around her neck.

"Oh, that's nothing," Viv said, tucking the futuristic device under her shirt and out of view. She pointed to the sidewalk chalkboard sign.

"What's the Ernest?" Viv asked.

"You don't know? It's far out!" he said, blowing out a ring of smoke. "The grooviest drink of the year, man! And I should know. I created it!"

"You're the bartender here?" Charlotte asked.

"Yes! Outta sight, right?"

"Why'd you name it 'the Ernest'?" Viv probed. "That's my dad's name! He's the guy we're looking for!"

"Oh! Far out, man!" the bartender said, leaning even far
ther back against the wall. "Now that you say it, you do look a
little like him."

"So, you've seen him?" Viv asked, a glimmer of hope
sneaking into her voice.

"Yeah, I've seen him! Ernest is one cool cat. Shows up here
every now and then. I named the drink after what he orders:
a special kind of cocktail. The secret?" The bartender leaned
down until he was at Viv's height and whispered into her ear.
"It's got vintage rum in it! A stellar spirit all the way from
1744."

He straightened up and pulled off his sunglasses for a better look.

"That's where I've seen that necklace before! Ernest wears
the same one every time he comes in. It's totally radical!"

So he still has his temporal transporter. Maybe we can use
that somehow to find him.

"But poor Ernest never sticks around for too long. Seems
like he's in some sort of trouble," the bartender continued.

"What do you mean?" Charlotte asked.

"This weird group of guys always barges in and seems to
chase him out."

"Weird guys? Weird in what way?" Viv asked.

The bartender looked up and down at the strange gaggle
of kids in front of him.

"A bit weirder than you," he said. "Everybody always

makes fun of me. They say I'm making up stories. But I've seen 'em. The man sends his spies all over the place looking to cause trouble."

"Could you describe them?" Viv asked.

The bartender tapped on his cigarette and brushed a drop of sweat from his brow.

"You kids sure are asking a lot of questions. You're not working for the man, too, are you?"

"Do we look like we're working for the man?" Charlotte crossed her arms.

The bartender looked over their modern clothes.

"Actually, yes. Yes, you do."

"Sir, I promise you," Viv said. "I'm just a kid looking for my dad. Nothing else. No funny business."

The bartender snuffed out his cigarette on the building and brushed his hands off on his pants.

"Well, you didn't hear it from me," he said. "But here's the skinny: Seems that every time Ernest comes around looking for a drink, he's followed. A group of three, all dressed in these dorky robes. One boy, one man, and an older geezer. Seems like Ernest must owe them money or something."

Wait, what the heck?

"A boy, a man, and an old geezer?" Viv asked.

"With all the man's spies runnin' around these days, ya never know. Seems like your dear old daddio might be on the lam," the bartender said. "Anyway, I gotta peace out back to the bar. You little flower children be careful out there."

And with that, he turned on his heels and walked into the lively establishment.

"Well, now what?" Charlotte asked.

"You heard that guy!" Viv said. "My dad likes vintage rum from 1744. Maybe that's one of the points in the loop!"

"We're leaving already?!" Ray complained.

"Sorry, Ray," Viv said. "We gotta catch up to my dad."

"But my tummy just settled down!" Ray said.

"Do you have any better ideas?"

Viv led her friends back to the alley where the time machine was parked, being sure to hop over the pile of puke on the sidewalk. A few rats scurried by as they made their way past a row of dumpsters. Viv jumped into the open time machine and motioned for her friends to follow. Charlotte and Elijah hopped in right behind her, but Ray rubbed his hands together nervously in the alleyway.

"Come on!" Viv beckoned.

"I don't know, guys," Ray said. "Maybe we should just wait here until your dad comes back?"

"We have no idea when he could loop back to this point!" Viv said.

"You wanna spend a few years with your new friend there?" Charlotte asked, pointing toward the ground. Down by Ray's feet, a little rat chewed at his shoelaces.

"AGH!" Ray said with a flailing kick. "Okay, let's go!"

Ray hobbled into the time machine and shut the doors behind him. Viv scrolled down on the trackpad through the time loop until she landed on the coordinates for the point in 1744.

"There!" she said. "Looks like our next destination is loaded up."

"But how do we power up the time machine without the control panel at the base?" Elijah asked.

A beeping came from each of their necks. Viv reached into her shirt and pulled out the necklace. The green digits on their temporal transporters flashed in a rhythmic tempo.

"Maybe . . . ," Viv said, turning the dial on her necklace until the numbers matched up to the coordinates on the dashboard.

Elijah and Charlotte followed suit, but Ray was hesitant.

"Come on, Ray!" Viv said. "We're wasting time!"

"I don't know, guys," Ray said. "I have a very delicate disposition—"

"RAY!" everyone shouted together.

"Okay! Fine!" Ray turned the dials on his transporter until they lined up with everyone else's. All of a sudden, a crackle of electricity passed through the interior of the time machine.

"Aw geez, here we go again!" Ray cried out.

The roar of the time portal blasted through the machine again, pulling the four kids into their next chrono-gateway.

CHAPTER SIX

Viv did a somersault off the top of the pile. Her arm felt like it had been asleep for hundreds of years. Ray somehow ended up on the bottom of the stack again, with Meekee even more squished beneath him.

"Meekee!" the little alien cried out, squirming beneath him on the floor of the time machine. The steam collected in a huge pool on the ceiling.

"Are we dead?" Ray asked, holding a hand to his head.

"Shh. Do you feel that?" Viv said.

Beneath their feet, a slight swaying tilted the entire time machine back and forth. Left and right.

"Are we . . . still traveling through time?" Ray asked.

Ray looked just as sick as before. The queasiness was even starting to get to Viv. She examined the dashboard one more time, making sure that the geographical coordinates and the chronological coordinates all still matched.

It looks like it worked.

"It almost feels like we're on a . . . ," Viv said.

She pulled the lever by the door, and the steel slats slowly slid open.

"Boat."

Just outside the doors of the time machine, a horde of pirates pointed a myriad of weapons directly toward the pack of shivering kids. Muskets, sharpened bayonets, and what looked like a hundred rusty swords all inches from their faces.

Behind them, a wooden mast extended toward a bright blue sky. Fluttering in the breeze was a black flag adorned with a foreboding sigil: a green, bony seahorse.

A heavily bearded man tottered forward from the huddle of ramshackle sailors. His peg leg matched the old wood of the deck, a prickly-looking dark cedar. He wore a leather tricorn hat littered with singed holes.

"Arr, matey! Don't ye move a muscle!" he called out through gnarled, rotten teeth. Viv could smell his stinky breath from ten feet away.

The kids put their hands up defensively. A bright red macaw sat on the man's shoulder, staring with beady eyes at the kids as they raised their hands in surrender.

"I be the cap'n o' this here vessel," he said. "An' ye lily-livered bilge all be uninvited guests on the *Em'rald Lady*."

"Are they speaking English?" Ray whispered.

"Aye! I be speakin' English, ye landlubbin' knave! An' me hearin' be jolly, too! Speak, ye!" the captain commanded.

"SQUAWK! Speak, ye!" The parrot on his shoulder echoed his words with a shrill screech.

There was a stunned silence until . . .

"Meekee?" the little alien pipped in response as he took his spot atop Ray's shoulder.

"Meekee, no!" Ray tried to push the little alien back down into his shirt pocket. But it was too late. A wave of gasps washed over the slack-jawed crew.

Viv stepped in front of Ray, guarding the sight of Meekee from all the prying eyes.

"Ernest," she said slowly. "Do you know a man named Ernest? We're looking for him."

"Aye? Ernest?" the captain said, squinting around at the other sailors. The man to his left gave a suspicious scowl.

Viv took a step forward, prompting another ripple of prodding swords straight to her throat. She gulped down a wad of spit.

"Yes. We're looking for—"

"Ahoy, matey!" Charlotte said, sliding in front of Viv.

"Char, what the heck are you doing?" Viv hissed.

"Let me handle this." Charlotte cleared her throat and spoke with her booming Frank voice. "Avast, 'ave ye spied a swashbuckler by the name o' Ernest Becker?"

The captain raised his bushy eyebrow. A bug crawled out of his hat and disappeared into his tangled, shaggy beard. Viv tried not to cringe.

"Ernest Becker, ye say?" he said, stroking his beard. He reached down and scratched an itch on his peg leg. "Wha' interests ye about dis Ernest Becker?"

"He been missin' fer a long time. 'Ave ye spied 'im?" Charlotte asked.

The captain took a few paces forward, his peg leg rapping against the ship's deck with every limping step.

"Let's say I 'ave spied this here Ernest Becker . . . ," the captain said. "An' let's say, fer instance, 'e left a scroll 'ere fer anybody lookin' fer 'im."

He left a scroll? Did he know we'd be coming?

"A scroll?" Viv asked. "If you could give us the scroll, we'll be on our way!"

"But the riddle remains," the captain continued. "Wha' good does it do me t' give it t' ye?"

"Are ye lookin' t' make a trade?" Charlotte asked.

"Aye, s'pose I be," the captain said.

"What be it that ye want?"

"'Ow about that there fancy ship ye used t' board us?"

Charlotte looked back at the time machine.

"Sorry, we can't give ye dis . . . uh . . . ship, matey. We be needin' that there vessel to sail homeward."

The captain stroked his beard again. "Ye've gotta funny-lookin' parrot there," he said, pointing straight toward Ray's shirt pocket.

Meekee growled at the pirate.

"Aye, he's a mighty rare bird," Charlotte said with pursed lips.

"Tell ye what," the captain said. "I'll give ye the scroll if ye give us the three-eyed green parrot."

"SQUAWK! Green parrot! Green parrot!" the red macaw on his shoulder cried.

"Meekee no parrot! Meekee no parrot!" Meekee said.

The captain bent down right at eye level with Ray.

"Aye, and 'e chatters, too. Betcha 'e would fetch a high price o' gold doubloons at the market."

Charlotte considered it for a few moments and then stuck out her hand for a shake.

"Sounds like ye got yerself a bargain, matey!"

"What?!" Ray shouted, pulling Meekee closer to his chest. "Charlotte? No way! No WAY! We are not trading Meekee!"

Before he could protest any further, Charlotte plucked Meekee out of Ray's hands and mouthed the words *trust me* to Ray.

"Ray!" Meekee said, reaching out all four of his little legs toward his best friend.

"Meekee!" Ray cried out, tears beginning to sting his eyes.

The captain perched Meekee on top of his open shoulder. Instantly, Meekee swung a little green punch at the macaw behind the captain's head.

"SQUAWK! Bad bird! Bad bird!" the parrot screeched.

The captain let out a hearty guffaw. "Yarr! A feisty one! I jus' might keep ye fer meself!"

Charlotte snapped her fingers. "Aye, 'ow 'bout that there scroll?"

Ray sniveled behind her. The captain nodded and gave a snicker to his crewmates. He reached into his coat jacket and pulled out a dripping clump of folded paper.

"What the—?" Charlotte cried, carefully unfolding the wafer-thin wad. Viv, Elijah, and Ray crowded around to read it. The ink on the paper ran slick with seawater. A series of dribbling numbers leaked across the page.

"Oy, you scoundrel! This here thin' be barely legible!" Charlotte complained.

"Aye! Din't say it'd be a dry scroll!" the captain jeered. "Bit tough t' keep anythin' dry on a pirate's ship!"

Charlotte fumed. She handed the scroll to Viv, and in one fluid motion, she lunged at the captain, swiping Meekee off his shoulder. The captain raised his sword higher in outrage, but before he could respond, a voice shouted from high above.

"AVAST!"

Every sailor snapped their head toward the sky. Viv squinted up at the hot Caribbean sun. Nestled in the crow's nest high up in the mast, a scraggly pirate pointed his long, bony arm toward the horizon.

"INCOMIN'! OFF THE PORT SIDE!"

A high-pitched whistling sound pierced the air. Mere seconds later, a small, round object soared through the open sky, beelining straight toward the ship.

"Watch out!" Viv said, grabbing Elijah and rolling toward the starboard railing.

The cannonball smashed into the deck, sending splinters and shrapnel flying into the air.

Four of the sailors fell through the hole in the deck, right into the galley below. A load of sizzling gruel exploded from the massive vat burning on the coal stove.

"We be under attack!" the captain screamed. "Man yer battle stations! Load the cannons, ye lazy scallywags!"

The chaos scattered the ship's crew across the poop deck. Charlotte and Ray tumbled forward toward the bow. Viv and Elijah scrambled to their feet and held each other in their arms.

Another enemy cannonball tore through the flag, ripping the green seahorse into pieces and leaving burn marks on the bits of fabric that remained.

Just one of those things could kill us!

Part of Viv wanted to reach out her arms, use her powers, and create a force field to protect them all. But with Elijah and Ray right next to her, the idea of revealing her alien side seemed worse than being hit by a cannonball.

I can't. I can't do it!

"Who's attacking us?!" Elijah shouted.

Viv spotted a collapsible brass telescope rolling down the deck, and she darted over quickly to grab it. She lifted it to her eye and peered through the clouded lens, locking her sights onto the opposing boat looming on the horizon. The enemy ship's deck was crawling with pirates. They scurried around like a colony of ants. But one shorter figure, standing as still as a statue on the bow of the ship, caught her attention—a young boy, no older than five or six, by the looks of him.

What the . . . ?

He was clothed in a long, white robe. Suddenly, despite being hundreds of yards away, the boy locked eyes with Viv through the telescope, as if he could see her, too!

"Agh!" she yelled, dropping the brass tube. The vintage glass shattered against the hard wood of the deck.

"CANNONBALL!"

Another lead projectile smashed into the side of the ship, delivering a devastating blow to the central mast. The skinny pirate who had been on lookout duty in the crow's nest came tumbling down, barely catching his feet in a tangle of ropes, leaving his head dangling mere inches above the deck. The entire ship shook like an earthquake.

"Fire in de hole!" a fellow sailor called out. Eruptions blasted out of the gunports on the starboard side of the boat.

"Let's get out of here!" Elijah shouted.

He grabbed Viv by the wrist and pulled her toward the

time machine, which was now threatening to slide off the deck into the exposed hull of the ship.

Charlotte and Ray leapt over the fractured barrels of gunpowder and ducked under the falling sheets of the sails, making their way toward their only chance at safety.

That deadly whistle zipped through the air again. Viv's head snapped up, pinpointing the fast-approaching projectile in the air.

It was a cannonball, and it was heading straight toward them.

"Viv!" Charlotte shouted. "Save us!"

No. NO.

In front of Ray? In front of Elijah?

"VIV!" Charlotte shouted.

There was no time to think. She had to make a split-second decision.

Her body, still exhausted and aching from her battle against the Chupacabra, fought to push her arms out in front of her. The power exploded from her hands. A green force field managed to catch the cannonball, slowing its trajectory in midair.

Viv's secret was out. No way to hide her alien powers from her friends now.

And even worse than that . . . her powers weren't strong enough. The velocity was too much for her weakened state to handle. The cannonball managed to creep along, still on a crash course to the time machine.

"I can't stop it!" Viv shouted, her head throbbing with pain.

I can't do this alone.

"Meekee!" Viv cried out. "Help me!"

The little alien instantly sprang into action. He leapt out of Ray's pocket and hovered in the air, releasing his trademark battle cry.

"MEEKEEEEE!"

His body glowed bright green as he lent his power to the force field Viv had already created. Together, the two managed to push the cannonball safely off course. It splashed into the ocean, sending a massive tidal wave slapping up against the surviving hunks of the ship.

"Quick! Get into the machine!" Charlotte instructed.

With her arms wrapped around Meekee, Viv ducked in through the doors. But Elijah and Ray were frozen, their eyes wide.

I knew it. They think I'm a monster.

Charlotte grabbed the boys by their wrists and yanked them in through the open doors. The ocean water poured in from all directions, gathering on the floor of the time machine as it started ever so slightly sinking.

The doors closed just as the water started to rush in.

No! This can't be happening! They weren't supposed to find out. Not like this!

BANG!

A piece of the ship pounded into the outside of the time machine, caving in a chunk of metal just a few inches above Ray's head.

But instead of screaming or jumping out of the way, Ray just blinked, staring at Viv like he'd just seen a ghost.

They hate me. They'll never trust me again.

BANG!

Another piece of debris slammed into the side of the time machine.

"Viv!" Charlotte shouted. "Let's go!"

Even the panic in Charlotte's voice wasn't enough to snap Viv out of her funk.

"Hello?" Charlotte said. "Is anyone listening?!"

Viv's head hung low, and she fiddled with the soaked scroll just to avoid looking at her friends' faces. The paper was so doused with seawater that the writing on it looked like a jumbled mess of ink.

"Let me see that!" Charlotte said, pulling at the scroll from Viv's hand. It immediately tore into two pieces.

"Oh, way to go, Charlotte!" Viv said, the flash of irritation a welcome reprieve from the fear.

"Boys?" Charlotte said. "Want to help out here?"

But Elijah and Ray were still stuck in a total stupor.

"All right! Guess I'll have to do everything!" Charlotte shouted. She reached over, adjusting the temporal transporters around Elijah's and Ray's necks. Stretching out across the time machine like a gymnast, Charlotte managed to twist the dials on Viv's device and the dashboard at the same time, allowing the portal to rip open and pull the four kids away from a watery demise just in time.

CHAPTER SEVEN

Even after the time jump, a bit of ocean water still lingered on the floor of the time machine, soaking everyone's feet down to their socks; everyone besides Meekee, who sat perched on top of a shivering Ray's shoulder. He and Elijah had backed up into one corner of the time machine.

Charlotte had been talking a mile a minute, explaining all the details that Viv had shared with her about her deepest, darkest secret. Viv hadn't been able to get any words out.

"And so now she has telekinetic powers but not, like, in a scary, evil, Megdar way," Charlotte finished.

Elijah and Ray were as stiff as boards. Their eyes blinked like they were communicating in Morse code.

Viv balled her fists down by her sides and braced for the worst. She fought off the urge to cry as the dented walls of the time machine suddenly felt like they were closing in even tighter.

I'm lucky Charlotte still has my back. Even Mom doesn't

know what to do with me. There's no chance Elijah will ever like me now that he knows the truth . . . He'll go running back to Joanna, even if she did let out everything in the Forbidden Zone!

Ray took a cautious step forward.

"So, you and Meekee . . . You can both move stuff with your minds?" Ray said.

Viv nodded, glad that this question was easy enough to answer.

"And you've had powers this whole time?" Elijah asked.

"Not the whole time. She didn't even know about them until last week," Charlotte defended. "Megdar's the one who explained how her mom had injected herself with his DNA without realizing she was pregnant with Viv!"

"Whoa, really?" Elijah said.

"It's true. Megdar told me on the spaceship when he tried to take me back to his planet," Viv explained.

It was quiet for a moment as the information washed over them. Ray scratched at the back of his head while Elijah let out a strong exhale.

They've been quiet for so long. If they're going to ditch me forever, I wish they'd just say it already.

"You're not going to hurt us, right, Viv?" Ray said. "I'm pretty delicate."

"No, of course not!" Viv said, feeling like she'd swallowed a cannonball. "Ray, it's still me."

"Guys, you don't have to be afraid," Charlotte said. "She's

totally in control of her powers. Right, Viv?"

Viv gave a nod that she hoped was convincing.

I wish I believed that . . .

"Wait, Viv, why did you only tell Charlotte?" Elijah asked.

"I caught her using her powers when we were in the Forbidden Zone," Charlotte said.

"Why didn't you tell us?" Ray said.

"It wasn't my secret to tell!" Charlotte said.

"No, I was asking Viv," Ray said. "Viv, why didn't you want us to know?"

Viv took a deep breath and tried to steady her voice. The trembling managed to break through, anyway.

"I was worried you'd think I was a freak," Viv said.

Elijah and Ray exchanged incredulous looks.

"A freak?" Ray said. "Are you kidding? I don't know if you remember, but my dad invented a fart gun, my best friend is a green alien, and I spent a good chunk of last week being fifty feet tall. If anyone's a freak, I don't think it's you."

"Yeah," Elijah added. "And Charlotte plays guitar with her feet. That's the freakiest thing I've ever heard of!"

"Hey!" Charlotte protested.

A laugh managed to escape through Viv's tears.

Am I dreaming? They actually don't care? Could it really be this easy?

"You're not a freak, Viv," Elijah said. "I think you're pretty darn awesome."

Viv blushed as she tried to stay steady on her feet. All of the anxiety, all of the nervousness that had been building up in the pit of her stomach suddenly felt like a knot beginning to unravel.

"Although," Ray said, "I kinda wished we had known a little earlier. Your powers could've really helped us out last night with all those creatures."

"Believe me, they did," Charlotte said, resting her arm proudly around Viv's shoulders.

Elijah let out a huff. "Wait, you were using your powers that whole time?!"

"Well, I mean yeah," Viv said. "At least, when you guys weren't around."

Elijah stepped forward, closing the tight space between them. He reached out and took Viv's hand in his.

"Viv? Is that how you saved my life last week?" Elijah asked. "When I was falling through the air in the terrarium?"

With pursed lips, Viv managed to nod her head. It felt like a lifetime ago that she had saved his life that way, back before she even realized she had powers.

Elijah squeezed her hand even tighter. "Then consider me your number-one fan."

Viv stared into his dark brown eyes, sensing his sincerity.

The knot unfurling in her stomach loosened again, finally making a little bit of room for the butterflies that seemed to swirl every time she looked into Elijah's eyes.

"There're so many things we can do with this!" Ray said. "Viv, you're a modern scientific marvel!"

"Well, I don't know about that," Viv said.

"Think about it! We could start a moving business! Or what about a theme park where all the rides are controlled by your mind? You could probably rob a bank if you really wanted to!"

Viv snorted. "Why would I want to rob a bank?"

"I dunno? Money! You're like . . . you're like a superhero! The sky's the limit!" Ray said.

"That's exactly what I said!" Charlotte exclaimed.

"Not as cute as Meekee but still pretty cool," Ray said.

Viv smiled and rubbed the tears out of her eyes. "So you don't think I'm a monster?" she asked.

"I mean, it is a little weird having a part-alien superhero friend," Ray said. "But nothing we can't handle!"

One final tear fell down Viv's cheek. Elijah reached out and brushed it away with his thumb.

"You're still the same Viv to me," he said. "I don't see you as any less human."

She felt a jolt of joy radiate from his smile. Her chest thundered as if the electricity in the time machine had zapped straight to her heart.

"Hey," Charlotte said. "Maybe you two can have your sweet moment when we're not all trapped in a soaking-wet time machine?"

"Aw geez, I almost forgot," Ray said. His nauseating burps returned with a vengeance.

"You know, you don't have to puke at every place we go," Charlotte said.

"I think the tank's empty." Ray patted his belly. "You know, guys, we can always just go back to our time."

"We're not leaving without Viv's dad," Elijah said. "Speaking of, where'd you send us, Charlotte?"

"To the place written down on that scroll the pirates had. I dialed us all to the same spot," Charlotte explained.

"Uh," Elijah said, hovering over the dashboard. "Are you sure? This doesn't even look like it's in the loop."

"What?" Charlotte pushed her way in front of the dashboard. Viv peered over her shoulder. Elijah was right. The floating point marking their time machine's coordinates was well outside of Ernest's loop.

"Oh great," Ray said. "Now we're actually lost?"

"It's not my fault that Viv ripped the scroll," Charlotte said.

"Oh, *I'm* the one who ripped the scroll?" Viv fired back.

"Careful, Charlotte!" Ray said. "Viv's got powers! She could throw you halfway across the galaxy if you're not careful!"

Viv stared back at him down the nosepiece of her glasses.

"That's not funny, Ray," Viv said. "Don't treat me like I'm any different."

"Sorry, sorry," Ray muttered, holding up his hands defensively.

"You better not make any more comments like that, or I'll fold you up into a pretzel with my mind," Viv said with a devious smile.

Maybe I could get used to this.

"Listen, I'm sorry about ripping the scroll, but it was either make a move or get pelted by cannonballs!" Charlotte said. "I'm sure those pirates are sitting at the bottom of the ocean by now. At least we're alive!"

I almost forgot.

"Guys, I saw something back there with the pirates," Viv said. "On the other ship that was shooting at us. There was this . . . kid."

"You could see all the way to that other ship?!" Ray exclaimed. "Is that part of your powers? Do you have, like, superhuman sight?"

"I used a telescope, Ray."

"Oh," Ray said. "Right."

"A kid? What about a kid?" Elijah pressed.

"I don't know," Viv said. "Something about him was . . . weird. He felt off."

"Was it his teeth? I can only imagine what it would be like growing up on a pirate ship," Ray said.

Charlotte fished through her pocket and pulled out the tattered pieces of the scroll.

"Forget the kid," she said, handing the wads of paper to Viv. "I sent the time machine to where these numbers said to go!"

Viv looked over the torn scroll, carefully holding the pieces back together. All the numbers were messy and impossible to read. It was a jumbled mess of ink and paper.

Viv reviewed the coordinates Charlotte had punched into the dashboard. They didn't line up with any of the points in her father's loop.

Oh no.

"Looks like we're not even on track with Ernest anymore. Charlotte, how could you tell with the ink running like that? What if that three is actually an eight?" Viv looked even closer. "Or that one is actually a seven?"

"Well, we're already here," Charlotte grumbled. "We might as well check!"

"Wait!" Ray said. "Be careful! Who knows what's outside that door!"

"Can you hear anything?" Elijah asked.

Charlotte pressed her ear up to the metal.

"Nope," she said. "It sounds mega quiet."

Viv pulled on the lever and the doors opened with a hiss. The inch or two of water collected on the floor poured out of the crack and spilled out onto a barren wasteland. Sharp rocks and a cavernous landscape stretched out as far as the eye could see. It was utterly silent.

Whoa . . . Are we still on Earth?

CHAPTER
EIGHT

The time machine had somehow landed wedged right between two rocky outcrops. Outside the doors, the landscape
was as arid and desolate as the desert surrounding Area 51.
But something about this terrain felt strange and foreign, certainly not like the grass-splotched valleys of Nevada. Wherever
they had landed, it was twilight, as the moon barely managed
to peek out through a wispy set of clouds.

Eventually, after a few minutes of watchful silence, Elijah
got out the first whisper. "I don't think anyone's here," he said.
"Charlotte must've put in the wrong coordinates."

"We should check just in case," Charlotte said. "Maybe
Ernest sent us here for a reason."

Charlotte took the first few steps out onto the rugged terrain, gently tiptoeing into a clearing, not daring to make a
sound.

Viv and Elijah were next. Ray and Meekee brought up the
rear. The entire area was perfectly silent.

"Dad?" Viv called out.

. . . DAD? . . . DAD? . . . DAD?

Her voice echoed across the rocky expanse and bounced back at them with an unusual distortion.

"Yikes, that's creepy," Ray said.

"Creepy! Creepy!" Meekee echoed.

Viv glanced at their surroundings. She couldn't shake the eerie feeling that someone or something was watching them.

This isn't right.

"There's no sign of Ernest anywhere," Elijah said. "Let's head back."

"Shh! Keep it down," Charlotte whispered. "Do you hear that?"

Viv looked around and hoped to see whatever it was Charlotte was sensing, only for something else to catch her attention. Down in the dust beneath her feet, a trail of footprints looped around the backside of the rocky cliff. But it wasn't just one set of footprints. It was dozens of them.

Oh no.

The sheer number of tracks would've been enough to freak her out. But it was the shape of the footprints that sent a shiver down her spine.

They looked strangely human . . . and yet, somehow not. The broad footprints were large and misshapen, with an extended big toe that stuck out at an uncomfortably wide angle.

Then, over the top of one of the ridges, Viv caught the first glimpse of who had been watching them. A head emerged just above the rock, covered in thick black hair. Like the footprints, it didn't look entirely human. Another head appeared right next to the first. Then another. And another, until the entire ridge was filled with sets of dark eyes glaring down at them. Slowly, the creatures climbed up atop the ridge, revealing just how muscular, intimidating, and hairy they really were. Viv felt Ray grip at her arm and squeeze.

"What . . . are those?" he whispered.

"They look like . . . monkeys? But they walk like humans?" Charlotte whispered.

"Any chance you speak ancient monkey, too?" Ray asked her.

"Um no," Charlotte said.

"They're apes," Elijah said.

"How can you tell?" Ray asked.

"No tail," Elijah pointed out. "Monkeys have tails. Apes don't."

Viv considered it for a moment.

Apelike humans? In an empty wasteland?

We must be really far back in the past.

"They must be early evolutionary versions of humans," she reasoned.

"If they're partly human, maybe they're friendly?" Elijah offered.

Worth a shot.

"Um, hello?" Viv said loudly enough for them to hear.

"UNGH! UNGH!" The first ape grunted at the sound of her voice.

"I'm not sure they've developed language yet," Elijah said.

"OOK-OOK! OOK-OOK!" The ape lifted an object high into the air above his head. The familiar oblong white shape could only be one thing.

A bone?

"EEEK-AAK-EEK!" The ape let out a terrifying screech.

The rest of the apes shrieked and hollered in a chorus.

"They don't sound friendly!" Ray yelped, squeezing Viv even tighter.

"And we're surrounded," Elijah said, looking toward the other ridge.

Another gathering of primates had grouped alongside the opposite ledge of rocks.

The other group of apes was quick to reply. They whooped in unison and howled at the opposing clan. Without warning, from both sides, the apes came roaring down the cliff in a furious tsunami of fur and beating chests. The two factions clashed in the middle of the clearing, slamming one another with their bony weapons.

"AHH!" Ray shouted as he jumped up into Viv's arms.

"At least they're not mad at us!" Charlotte said.

"Let's get the heck outta here before they change their minds!" Elijah said.

But before she could even take a step, Viv felt a shiver creep up her spine. Under the moonlight, beyond the rocky clearing, a flurry of dust moving through the air like a tornado caught her eye.

What the—?

"Guys? What's that?!"

The dust conglomerated into a form, a rather tall figure. Whatever it was materialized out of thin air. But it wasn't an ape. Beyond the warring creatures, the gliding figure ducked out of a shadowy nook beneath the far side of the rugged cliff and came into view. The silhouette was undeniable. It was a taller human figure, cloaked in a long, white robe.

That robe looks just like that boy's on the pirate ship!

The figure took a slow step forward. All four kids watched as the rock beneath its feet crumbled into sand with every stride.

"Uh, I don't think that's a monkey!" Viv said.

"Unless maybe he evolved really quickly?" Elijah suggested.

"Hey!" Viv shouted over the screeching ape noises. "You there!"

No response.

"Do you speak English?" Viv said. "Have you seen a man by the name of Ernest Becker?"

The man continued his slow march, inching closer to the clash of apes separating him from the kids.

"Don't come any closer!" Viv shouted.

But the man completely ignored her and took a few more menacing steps forward. And then a few more steps until he was just a few yards away.

"Hey! I'm warning you!" Viv said, lifting her hands.

A stray bone lying on the ground had been left by one of the fighting hominids. Viv tried to pick it up with her powers to show the cloaked figure she meant business. But it was no use. Her abilities were toast after stopping that cannonball.

Come on, Roswellian DNA! Now would be a good time to kick in!

Viv struggled as the bone rattled against the rock, only managing to lift it a few centimeters off the ground.

"Viv?" Elijah said. "I thought you said you could control your powers?"

"I swear, this never happens!" Viv said.

Or at least, almost never.

The man walked right between the warring factions. One of the apes approached him and reared back with a bone, ready to attack, but the man extended his hand from the robe. He placed his palm against the ape's face. Before Viv's very eyes, the ape transformed into sand, crumbling away to the ground.

What in the—?!

"Okay, he's *definitely* not friendly!" Ray shouted.

The man turned his attention back to the four kids. His

eyes were a sickly shade of pale yellow

"RUN!" Viv screamed.

The kids scrambled backward. Their feet pounded across the stony ground as they hustled back toward the time machine.

Short of breath and pumping her legs as fast as she could, Viv made the mistake of looking back over her shoulder. The robed man had burst into a full-blown sprint and was closing the distance on them.

Oh geez! He's fast!

Viv picked up the pace. The four kids barely made it to the open doors of the time machine, pushing one another in.

"Get inside! Get inside!" Viv yelled.

Ray was first. Viv shoved Elijah and Charlotte in just as the man reached out for a fistful of Viv's hair. At the last second, she spun on her heels, bashed down on the lever, and watched in horror as the doors to the time machine slammed shut—right onto the man's outstretched hand. The appendage broke off clean at the wrist and fell to the floor.

"AHH!" The kids let out a collective scream and scrambled toward the rear of the machine.

The hand twitched for a moment before disintegrating into sand, leaving a gritty pile on the floor.

"LET'S GET OUT OF HERE!" Elijah shouted.

"To where?!" Ray asked, squished up against the control panel.

"I don't care!" Charlotte said. "Just get us out of here, Ray!"

"I'm trying! I'm trying!" Ray said, slapping his hands down onto the control panel. He punched in a random coordinate and dialed the corresponding numbers into his temporal transporter.

"Meekee! Help!" he shouted.

Meekee lit up the dials on Charlotte's, Elijah's, and Viv's temporal transporters, perfectly matching the number set Ray punched in and—

CHAPTER NINE

Viv's eyes blinked open. Her atoms still vibrated from the recent transport. She rubbed at her forehead and picked herself up off the floor with a grunt.

"Did we just accidentally chop off a guy's hand? And it turned into sand? Or did I dream that?" Elijah asked, clutching at his back.

"No, I saw it, too," Charlotte said.

"And look," Viv said, pointing toward Ray. "There's the proof."

Somehow, in the midst of traveling through time, Ray had ended up face-first in the small pile of sand by the door.

"AGH!" Ray shouted. He jumped to his feet and began to ferociously brush himself off. "Aw geez! Why'd I have to land in that man's hand sand?!"

"Who the heck was that guy?" Charlotte asked.

"I don't know, but did you all see that robe he was wearing?" Viv said. "That was just like the long, white robe that bartender told us about. And the one that kid on the pirate ship was wearing!"

"Maybe that bartender hadn't just drunk one too many Ernests," Charlotte said. "Maybe your dad really is in some kind of trouble."

Why would those guys be after my dad?

"Whoever he was, that guy definitely did not belong there," Viv said. "And now that I think about it, neither did that kid on the pirate ship."

"Maybe they're time travelers, too?" Elijah offered.

Other time travelers? I hadn't even considered that . . .

"Speaking of . . . ," Viv said. "Ray? Where did you send us?"

"I—uh, I don't know," Ray said. "I punched in something random so we could get out of there!"

Viv examined the dashboard. Their green speck of light was just a few ticks off from the ring marked "E. Becker."

"Oh man, looks like we're even further back in the past," she said. "But . . . we are closer to my dad's loop!"

"See? You guys can always trust good ol' Ray!" he said with a smile.

Viv considered it for a moment.

That might not be a bad idea . . .

"Okay, from this moment on, Ray, you're in charge of plugging coordinates into the dashboard," Viv said.

"What?!" Charlotte cried. "You're putting Ray in charge?"

"Roger that, Captain!" Ray said with a salute. "As a lifelong time travel enthusiast, you can count on me!"

"Why Ray? Why not me?" Charlotte asked.

"Um, because last time I checked, you were the one who took us to scary monkey town?" Ray argued.

"Ugh. Fine."

And with that, Ray pulled down on the lever, and the doors slid open.

Warm, tropical light poured into the time machine in a thousand shades of orange and yellow. Palm trees towered overhead and coastal grass swayed in the breeze. A gentle ocean tide rolled in just a few yards down the shore.

A beach?

"Wow. Great call, Ray!" Elijah said. "It's beautiful here."

"Not sure I'm really excited to see any more sand, but I guess this will do." Ray gave a smug smile and motioned for the others to step out.

Elijah was right. It was absolutely gorgeous. The water was a crystalline blue, and huge flowers bloomed along the shoreline.

But the real magnificent sight was the sunset, a bright orange glow that filled the sky with a stunning display of colors.

"Guys?" Charlotte said as they walked along the shore. "Is it just me, or is that sunset getting closer to us?"

Viv shielded her eyes from the light and squinted toward the horizon. Charlotte was right. The light was getting bigger.

And brighter . . . and . . . fiery?

"Uh—that's not a sunset," Viv said.

"What is it then?" Ray asked.

Elijah had clearly figured out the same thing. "It's an asteroid!"

The tropical climate. Being this far back in time.

"That's not just *an* asteroid . . . It's *the* asteroid!" Viv said, putting it all together. "We're in the Yucatán Peninsula, circa sixty-six million years ago!"

"Oh crud," Ray said. "First the dinosaurs. Now us!"

"Get back in! Get back in!" Viv called out.

The four kids sprinted across the sand back toward the time machine. A flock of pterodactyls flew overhead, racing to escape the incoming doom. The massive asteroid had entered the lower layers of the atmosphere and was now a fireball hurtling directly to the shore where the time machine was planted.

Ray flopped his hands down on the dashboard as Charlotte shut the doors behind them. He called out the numbers of their destination. Everyone followed suit, spinning the dials on their temporal transporters until they all matched up.

"Hold on!" he shouted.

"Viv? Viv?" Elijah said. "You okay?"

Viv opened her eyes. She was still lying on the floor of the time machine.

"Wh-where are we?" Viv asked.

"Ray sent us through another portal," he said. "Look."

The doors were already open. Elijah helped Viv to her feet as she peered out into their new location.

It was a quaint ancient town; European, by the looks of it. A paved stone road extended out down a row of richly decorated homes. Fountains and sculptures sat on every corner, and a beautiful marble veneer coated all the pillars.

"This isn't so bad, right?" Ray said, running his hands through his moppy mess of hair.

"I think my parents have been here before," Charlotte said. "I swear, they have travel pictures from a place just like this . . ."

A woman in a long, white tunic with a belt tied around the waist passed by carrying a basket full of figs. She gave the strange machine and the group of children a twisted look.

"Excuse me, ma'am? Is there anything around here that could potentially kill us?" Ray questioned.

The woman shook her head, mumbled a few words in Latin, and continued walking.

Viv looked down at her temporal transporter and interpreted the long string of numbers.

"Seventy-nine BC . . . ," Viv said. "Why does that sound so familiar?"

A distant vibration shook the ground.

"Hey, look!" Ray said. "This place even comes with its own rumbling mountain!"

Oh crud!

"That's Mount Vesuvius!" Viv exclaimed.

"Mount Ve-what?" Ray asked.

Families and people came bursting out of their homes. They sprinted down the mountainside, running for cover.

"We're in POMPEII!" Viv shouted.

Hot lava and ash spewed out of the mouth of the volcano, erupting in a vertical column that stretched for miles up in the air.

The kids rushed back into the time machine. Viv clung to the wall, trying to slow her breathing. Flying rocks and smoke filled the sky as the debris began to rain down. She slammed on the lever and shut the doors.

"RAY!" Elijah yelled. "Let's get a move on!"

"Preferably somewhere that won't kill us, please!" Viv said.

"I really don't think Ray should be in charge!" Charlotte screamed.

"Wait, wait! One more try!" Ray said, twisting the dials on his temporal transporter.

The doors to the time machine opened to a horribly foul

stench. It was a medieval city—Britain in 1348, according to the dashboard.

People moaned and limped through the streets. Nearly everyone seemed to be infected with a horrific disease. Huge, bulbous lumps protruded from their exposed skin. This time, the kids didn't even dare to step out.

"That's the bubonic plague, isn't it?" Ray said.

"Yep," Viv said.

She pulled down the lever and shut the doors.

"Does anybody have antibacterial soap on them?" Ray asked.

Charlotte twisted around to Ray, grabbed him by the collar, and lifted him a foot clean off the ground.

"Are you trying to get us killed?" she screamed.

"I'm sorry! I'm sorry!" Ray yelled back.

"No! Ray good! Ray smart!" Meekee cried.

"Ray dead meat if he doesn't clean up his act!" Charlotte said with a glare in Meekee's direction.

"Charlotte, put him down!" Viv said, studying the dashboard. "Okay, new plan. Ray, you're hereby relieved of your navigational duties. Let me give it a whirl."

She cracked her knuckles and ran some calculations in her head, trying to decipher from the row of twenty-five splotchy digits which number combinations they hadn't tried yet. There was only one possible option left that would match up with any of the points on Ernest's loop.

"Okay. If I'm right, this should set us back on the path," Viv said.

She walked over to Charlotte and twisted the dial on her temporal transporter, matching up the numbers with their destination. Ray was next. Then Elijah.

"Where we off to next, Captain?" Elijah asked with a wink. Viv smiled back at him.

"How does Ancient Egypt sound?"

The heat hit Viv like a ton of scorching-hot bricks. She felt like she was in an oven the instant the doors opened. On the dashboard, she saw what she'd been desperately hoping to see: Their green point on the map lit up right along the loop marked "E. Becker."

"It worked!" she said. "We're back on track!"

"That's ace, mate!" Charlotte cheered.

"That means he's gotta have been here . . . ," Viv said.

"Maybe over there?" Elijah asked, pointing at the three gargantuan pyramids towering above the sand.

Wow. The Pyramids of Giza! They're even more impressive in person.

Viv's amazement was cut short. They weren't out there alone. Over a nearby dune, a group of ancient Egyptians dressed in linen skirts and fine, pleated robes traversed the desert with ease.

"Shh," Viv whispered. "Stay quiet. There's a group of people right over there!"

"I think I'm gonna puke again," Ray said, staggering out of the time machine. He took a dozen dizzy paces forward before falling to his hands and knees in the sand.

"You've gotta be kidding me," Viv said.

"Uh-oh, Ray," Charlotte said. "Vomiting is a symptom of the bubonic plague, ya know."

"NO!" Ray cried. "Is it really? I have a very weak immune system!" He was doubled over and just about to hurl when Meekee pipped from his shoulder.

"Ray! Ray! RAY!" Meekee cried.

"Meekee, hush!" Viv whispered. "We can't risk anybody seeing you!"

Before anybody could stop him, Meekee jumped into action. His entire body glowed with a bright green aura. The force field enveloped Ray and lifted him high into the air.

"Meekee! What are you doing?!" Ray yelled, his limbs flailing below him.

A few inches from where Ray had been crouched, a hissing Egyptian cobra slithered away through the sand.

Crud. That was almost bad.

Meekee managed to reposition Ray safely back on the ground away from the retreating serpent, but it was too late. All the shouting had garnered the attention of the Egyptians over the dune's ridge. They made their way across the sand at an alarmingly fast pace.

"Should we run?" Elijah asked, jabbing his thumb back toward the time machine.

"No!" Viv said. "We're finally back in my dad's loop."

We gotta stand our ground. Maybe they know something.

The Egyptians closed in on them in a matter of seconds. They moved with acute precision across the sand, circling Ray and Meekee like a swarm of vultures.

"No! Please don't hurt Meekee!" Viv begged. "He's our friend! He's harmless!"

Charlotte and Elijah stood behind her, trying their best to cover the time machine with their bodies. But the Egyptians sped right by Meekee, instead scooping Ray from the sand and lifting him up high on their shoulders.

"What the—?" Viv said. "They don't even care about Meekee?"

"It's almost like they've seen aliens before . . . ," Elijah said.

"Hey! Give him back!" Charlotte yelled. "That's our nerd!"

The Egyptians took off toward the pyramids, with Ray thrashing wildly above their outstretched arms.

"Help me!" Ray called out.

The group of Egyptians carrying him began to chant.

"Ra . . . Ra . . . Ra . . . Ra . . . Ra . . ."

"No, I'm Ray!" the flailing boy cried out.

"I think they think you're Ra!" Viv said as they ran to keep up with the crowd. "The Egyptian god of the sun and sky!"

"What?! Why?!" Ray cried.

"I mean, your name is Ray, and they did see you hovering above the sand," Charlotte said. "It's an understandable mistake."

Viv, Elijah, Charlotte, and Meekee hustled alongside the pack of seasoned sand travelers, but trudging through the Sahara in sneakers proved harder than they'd expected.

"My name is Ray! Ray Diamond Mond!" the boy pleaded, his voice growing fainter with each step. "Not Ra!"

After a few minutes of trudging through the sand, the Egyptians disappeared with Ray into the stone mouth of a temple outside the pyramids. Sweating and huffing, the kids followed a good thirty seconds behind.

Once they ducked below the doorway, Viv was stunned by what she saw. Inside, a larger group of Egyptians waited with a palanquin. Like an orchestrated dance, they scooped Ray from the hands of those carrying him and placed him onto the cloth-draped platform. They paraded him around the gathered mass of people, all bowing and reaching out their hands to touch the mystical boy-embodiment of their god. The women decorated Ray with fine gold jewelry. The men fanned him with large palm fronds, offering him bowls of grapes.

The three kids stuck close to the wall by the entrance, trying to stay out of sight.

"Well, if I'm being honest, I don't think Ray's in any real danger," Elijah whispered.

"Unless this is one of those 'treat him like a king, fatten him up, and eat him later' kind of scenarios," Charlotte added.

Viv scanned their surroundings, looking for anything that could help them avoid Ray getting gobbled up like a roasted luau pig.

The walls of the temple were covered in breathtaking hieroglyphics. Viv ran her hand along the limestone, feeling every groove and notch of the fine carvings. Her fingers couldn't keep up with her eyes as she surveyed the massive expanse of emblems. But one corner of the wall looked out of place. She rubbed the sand out of her glasses and squinted until the characters became clear.

Oh my gosh. This is huge!

"Guys!" Viv said, nudging Charlotte and Elijah. "Look at those hieroglyphics!"

The two surveyed the area of the wall she was pointing at.

"What? The one that looks like a lion with lightning coming out of its butt?" Charlotte asked.

"No, not that one! Those ones!"

Among the ornate hand-drawn symbols of birds, snakes, and objects, there was a long list of numbers and then a group of Roman alphabet letters:

ERNEST B

"He was here!" Viv said. "And those must be the coordinates for where he wants us to go!"

She repeated the numbers in her head over and over again,

turning them into a little song: a trick her mom had taught her during her earliest days in kindergarten.

"Then what are we waiting for?" Elijah said. "Let's grab Ray and go!"

The bearers of the palanquin were circling back around to the entrance of the temple. Viv, Charlotte, and Elijah scurried up through the crowd until they were just a few feet away from Ray.

"Hey, Ra," Charlotte said. "Get off your high horse. Come on, we're getting outta here."

"I dunno, guys. Surprisingly, I really like it here," Ray said, popping another fistful of fruit into his mouth.

"Stop filling up on grapes, you doofus!" Charlotte said. "You're just gonna puke them up later!"

"Maybe I could stay here for a little bit while you guys figure out all the Ernest stuff," Ray suggested. "I deserve a little ancient Egyptian vacation."

The palanquin bearers began another lap around the temple. Viv surveyed the crowd ready to receive their new boy-god. An old man trailed from the back corner of the temple, heading closer and closer to Ray. He looked unusual compared to the rest of the Egyptians. Instead of the linen skirts and beaded tops worn by the other Egyptian congregants, a heavy robe hung on his limbs. The robe was stark white.

Old man? White robe?

A hand-painted vase sat on a nearby pedestal, decorated

with a beautiful scene of the pharaoh and his queen. In one smooth motion, Viv grabbed the vase off its stand and chucked it straight toward the old man. It soared across the room, sending gasps and panic through the worshipping Egyptians. Instinctively, the elderly man cowered, with his hand covering his face. The second it made contact with his arm, the entire vase crumbled into a pile of sand.

Uh-oh.

"He's one of them! RUN!" Viv yelled.

From up on the platform, Ray had seen it, too.

"Okay, I'm ready to go now!" he said. He leapt off the palanquin, flinging gold and jewels around the temple. The Egyptians gasped at the sight of their newfound deity sprinting across the floor like a wounded badger.

"Ra! Ra! Ra!" they shouted.

The four kids hightailed it out of the granite entryway, dashing through the thick sand as best they could. The Egyptians gave chase, shouting and cursing in their ancient-sounding language. Behind them, the older man had broken out into a sprint, too, and they were all covering ground faster than the kids had hoped.

"We're not close enough!" Charlotte said. "They're gonna catch us!"

"Viv! Meekee!" Ray said. "Do something!"

The little alien exploded with a massive aura of green light, extending it toward the time machine and encasing the entire device in his field. With a few grunts, he managed to drag the time machine across the dune, leaving a long trail in the sand. The doors opened, and the kids piled in just before the ancient Egyptians could reach them. A flurry of fists banged on the doors.

Without a second to waste, Viv recited the newly memorized song in her head, plugged the coordinates from the hieroglyphics wall into the dashboard, and turned to her friends with a fearless smile.

"It's time to find my dad."

CHAPTER TEN

Viv could feel the gritty bits of sand caked in her ears. Slowly but surely, the four kids worked their way up onto their feet, brushing the traces of Egypt off their clothes. Meekee's exhausted little body huffed and puffed, collapsing onto the dashboard of the time machine in a weary heap.

Charlotte folded her arms and zeroed in on Ray.

"Ray?" Charlotte said. "Back there, did you say your middle name is Diamond?"

"Yeah?" he said.

"So, your full name is Raymond Diamond Mond?" Charlotte asked.

Ray gave a shrug.

"Boy, your family has quite the taste in names, huh?" Charlotte laughed.

"I don't know. I kind of like it. You know what they say. Diamonds are forever," Elijah said.

"They're also a girl's best friend," Ray said, draping his

arm around Charlotte's shoulders

"Not in your wildest dreams, buddy," Charlotte scoffed. She pushed him off with a hearty shove, sending Ray flying back toward the doors.

"Where are we now?" Elijah asked.

Without warning, the doors to the time machine slid open. Ray lifted his hands up, indicating that they were nowhere near the lever.

"Did you open the doors?" Viv said.

"No? They just opened by themselves," Ray replied.

The vapor from inside the machine came pouring out in a misty fog. Once it cleared, the scene outside was instantly recognizable.

"Aw, man," Elijah said. "We're back at Area 51?"

The Continuum Navigation wing looked nearly the same as the way they'd left it.

"We must've messed something up," Elijah said. "Did we loop back around to the present?"

"No way," Viv said. "I put in the coordinates Ernest etched into the pyramid."

"Are you sure you got the numbers right?" Elijah said.

"I think so?" Viv replied.

It was a lot of numbers . . . Maybe I missed one?

"Why would he send us home?" Ray asked.

Charlotte stepped out of the doors and into the hall. The whole place was empty and entirely quiet.

"Mom?" Charlotte said. "Dad? We're back!"

She spun around on her heels and inspected the room.

"Guys, look," she said. "Something's different here."

Viv, Elijah, and Ray stepped out alongside her, examining the place where their journey had begun.

She was right. Along the outer edges of the room, instead of the broken-down, rusty time machines, rows of shiny, new contraptions lined the walls.

"What the—? Have they been building new time machines while we were gone?" Elijah asked.

Viv ducked her head and climbed back into the time machine. She shuffled over to the dashboard and scrolled through the coordinates until their point lit up on the map.

"This says we're in . . . 2050?" she said.

The realization washed over each of the kids, one by one.

"The *future*?" Ray said. "Whoa. No way!"

"But if we're in the future, wouldn't that mean—" Charlotte began but was cut off by a noise from the back of the room. Instinctively, the four kids huddled together, prepared for whatever levels of craziness this future version of Area 51 had in store for them.

It was the doors, now fixed from Director Harlow's plasma blast, sliding open. A tall woman dressed in a smart pantsuit stepped out, followed by three other people. They smiled and waved at the kids, closing the distance between them. The sight of them nearly took Viv's breath away.

It can't be,

The woman looked practically identical to her mother. The same streak of gray ran through her hair. But she looked younger than Viv had ever seen her. For a moment, Viv considered that perhaps they had invented an antiaging serum at the base, something that had frozen her features in time.

". . . Mom?" Viv asked.

The woman let out a huge guffaw of a laugh.

"No, not quite," she said, taking a few assured steps forward. The shortened distance gave Viv an even clearer view of the features on her face. The black-framed glasses. The tiny dimples in her smile. The woman's true identity hit her like a ton of bricks.

"Viv, it's me," the woman said. "You. I'm Viv. We're both Viv."

No. Freaking. Way.

Viv felt the grip of her friends tighten around her.

"You're . . . *me*?" Viv asked.

"Well, technically, I go by Vivian now," she said. "But yes! It's me in the flesh. Well, you in the flesh. Both of us in the same flesh, I suppose. That sounds weird, doesn't it?"

Viv's mouth hung open like a fish on a hook. A stutter got tangled up on her tongue as she tried to get out a response.

"S-s-so you're me . . . in the future?" she said.

"Kinda shocking, isn't it?" The older Viv smiled. "I remember the feeling."

"Then that means . . . ," Elijah said, pointing at the other three adults behind her. They each gave a friendly wave.

Now that Viv realized who she was looking at, their identities were unmistakable. The older Elijah exuded the same suave, effortlessly cool energy as his younger counterpart. In place of a smooth chin, a thick black beard covered the lower half of his face.

Next to him was Charlotte, all grown up. She'd somehow managed to grow even taller than her parents. Despite the fact that her long blond hair had been chopped short, she still had that indisputable twinkle of mischievousness in her bright blue eyes.

The older Ray, on the other hand, looked exactly the same. The same messy mop of hair sat proudly on the top of his head, yet not an ounce of facial hair had managed to creep in under his nose. The younger Ray stepped out from the pack of kids; his hands extended incredulously.

"You're kidding me," Ray said. "We didn't grow a single extra inch?"

"Believe me, buddy," Older Ray said. "I was just as disappointed as you."

"We knew you'd be coming," Older Elijah said.

"Really?" the younger Elijah said. "How?"

"Well, uh . . . because we are you," Older Charlotte said. "Let me guess. You guys just came from Egypt, right?"

The younger kids nodded in pure wonder.

"Yep, I remember that," Older Charlotte said. "Ray got scooped up and taken into that temple by the pyramids."

"You guys went through that, too?" Viv asked.

"Yep! Everything in your lives that has happened up until this point, all the same things happened to us when we were your age," Older Elijah explained.

Whoa. Time travel is wild.

Viv thought it over for a moment.

"So . . . that means another version of older us helped you guys when you were young?" she said.

"That's right," Older Viv said. "And it means that in 2050, when you guys are our age, you'll have to do the same thing to the younger versions of yourselves."

"Dang. My brain just exploded," Ray said.

"So does that mean Ernest is here?" Viv asked.

"Ernest?" Older Viv said. "No, unfortunately. At least not right now. He time jumped here a few years ago for fifty-two seconds. I think it's what convinced him to leave those coordinates back in Egypt. We haven't seen him since then. But the good news is, you're back on the right track!"

Viv observed every angle and detail of her counterpart's face. She couldn't help but marvel at the striking resemblance she'd one day share with her mom. She wondered if the resemblances extended beyond the physical as well—was this Older Viv the type of person who would keep the truth from her child?

Still . . . Wherever Mom is, I hope she's all right.

"What about Mom?" Viv said. "Is she okay?"

"Well, my mom and your mom are technically two different moms from two different timelines," Older Viv said. "Your mom? I assume she's still chasing after Dad in the time loop."

"And what about . . . your mom?" Viv asked.

"Yeah! Can you tell us anything about the future?" Elijah said.

Older Viv's face morphed into an uneasy expression.

"That's the thing," she said, fidgeting a bit. "As you all know, the timeline is extremely delicate. So, there's only a limited number of things we can talk about. Anything we tell you could alter our entire lives here in the future."

"Oh, come on!" Charlotte said. "Just tell us a few things!"

"Can you at least tell us who's going to win the next Super Bowl?" Ray asked.

"Oh, football was outlawed quite a long time ago," Older Ray said.

"Really?"

"Yep. It's now completely illegal. That was under President Zendaya, if I recall correctly."

"Wait a second, Zendaya got elected president?!"

"No, I'm just joking." Older Ray smirked.

The kids chuckled, until Older Ray raised an eyebrow.

"Or am I?"

"Quit teasing them, Ray!" Older Elijah said. "We don't have a lot of time. There are some important things we need to show you."

"I thought you said you can't tell us anything? So we don't mess up the timeline?" Viv said.

"We can only share the same information that was told to us when we were in your shoes," Older Viv explained.

She motioned to the lines of time machines along the walls.

"As you can see, we have a pretty good grasp on time travel now," she said. "We're able to control it much more easily in the future."

A gleaming twinkle of light sparkled on her hand, catching the younger Viv's eye. The placement and the sheer size of the diamond meant it could only be one thing.

"Is that . . . a ring on your finger?" Viv asked. "Are you married?"

"Oh shoot," Older Viv said, quickly tucking her arm around her back and out of sight. "I forgot to take that off."

"Vivian!" Older Charlotte scolded.

"I'm sorry!" she said stiffly.

"Who are you—I mean, who are *we* married to?!" Viv asked.

Older Viv exchanged a fleeting glance with Older Elijah.

Do we . . . end up together?

"I can't tell you anything," Older Viv said with a sigh.

"What?! Come on!" Ray cried. "If you can't tell us who we're married to, what about some winning lottery numbers?"

"We don't want anything to interfere with our timeline. The older version of ourselves we met all those years ago said the same thing," Older Elijah said.

"Listen, this isn't what's important right now. We don't have a lot of time," Older Viv said. "They'll be coming for you soon."

"They? Who's they?" Viv asked. "Are you talking about those weird sand dudes in robes? Cause we've been seeing them everywhere."

"We'll talk about that soon. But for now, it's crucial that everything goes along exactly according to plan," Older Viv said.

"Was that Zendaya joke according to plan?" Ray said.

"Actually, yes," Older Ray said, rubbing the back of his head with an air of embarrassment. "The older Ray from our timeline made the same joke."

"Well, that's a little disappointing," Ray said. "You stole comedic material?"

"Uh yeah," Older Ray replied. "From myself!"

"Anyway," Older Viv continued. "You're gonna need every bit of information we give you if you want to make it out of this thing alive."

"Really?" Charlotte said. "So that's it? You won't tell us anything about our personal lives?"

"The only thing I can tell you is that you all still work at Area 51," Older Viv said. The four adults each flashed the holographic employee badges floating by their hips.

"And, Viv—*you're* the new director."

CHAPTER
ELEVEN

Viv stood frozen like a deer in headlights. Elijah gave her a playful nudge.

"Director Vivian Harlow," he said. "Has a nice ring to it!"

"So . . . you're telling me that I work here for the next *thirty* years?" Viv asked.

After the week she'd just had, that prospect sounded utterly exhausting.

"Don't worry. Things get better. I promise. But right now, we don't have a lot of time. The cloaking system over the base will save us a few minutes, but let's not push it any further than we have to. Until then, we have a few gifts for you," Older Viv said. "Ladies and gentlemen, I present to you . . ."

She pulled out an adjacent drawer on the center table, revealing three small devices.

"The finest array of souvenirs from 2050 a kid could ask for!"

"What are those?" Charlotte asked.

"You mean you don't recognize them?" Older Viv said. "They're your trusty gadgets!"

"I guess you could say that we've made some upgrades over the last few decades," Older Charlotte added.

"I don't understand. Where's the flight suit?" Elijah asked.

"Oh, you're gonna love this," Older Elijah said. He reached in and pulled out a tiny orange orb, as smooth and glistening as a pearl. He handed it to his younger counterpart.

"*This* is the flight suit?" Elijah said, lifting up the minuscule device. "Where's the, um . . . suit part of it?"

"Welcome to the future, Elijah," his older version said with a smile. "With this, there's no need for jet fuel. Or wings, for that matter. The entire thing is powered completely by reverse magnetic propulsion, using the Earth's own geomagnetic field as a charging source. So as long as there's still an Earth, you'll be able to fly with this!"

"This thing? You're telling me that *this* thing can fly?" He held the pint-size device up to the light. It was no larger than a marble.

"Faster than an SR-71 and as quiet as a mouse," Older Elijah said.

"Whoa, that's so awe—"

"Got anything for me?" Charlotte butted in.

Older Charlotte stepped up to the drawer, removing what

looked like a necklace fashioned with a long golden chain and a ring of shimmering crystals.

"Ever get tired of carrying around those bulky duplicator gauntlets?" she said in an infomercial-style voice.

"Yes!" Charlotte replied.

"Ever wish you could use your hands *and* infinitely clone yourself at the same time?"

"Yes! Yes! Yes! Every day!" Charlotte was practically foaming at the mouth.

"Then may I introduce to you the brand-new, fully cognitively connected duplicator amulet!" She hung it around the younger Charlotte's neck. "It's linked to brain waves, so now you can clone anyone you want and control their copies. Well, as long as they have a brain."

"You're serious?" Charlotte said. "So I can clone anybody that I see and impersonate them?"

"That sounds dangerous," Viv said.

"Sounds like the perfect way to frame Ray for a crime!" Charlotte chimed in.

"Hey!" the two Monds protested at the same time.

"It's a lot of power and responsibility," Older Charlotte said. "So you need to be careful. But it's also a whole lotta fun!"

The younger Charlotte examined the pendant hanging on her chest.

"What about the crystals? Are they, like, magical copying stones?"

Older Charlotte gave a shrug. "I just thought they looked good! It's fashionable!"

Ray cleared his throat and stepped up to the drawer full of high-tech goodies. "Got anything in there that could help me bust out of jail if I was, oh I don't know . . . incriminated for a crime I didn't commit?"

"Ah, yes," Older Ray said. "Here we go. This is your growth ray."

He pulled out a small blue pistol. It looked nearly identical to Ray's original gadget, complete with the same growth and shrink buttons and block lettering etched into the side.

"What's the difference?" Ray asked.

"No difference," Older Ray said. "It's the exact same thing."

"Oh, come on!"

"What? I was busy working on other stuff!" the older Ray defended. "Like this!"

From his pants pocket, he pulled out a slim, dark gray rectangle and handed it over. The weight of the mysterious device nearly brought the younger Ray to the ground.

"Geez this is heavy! What is this? Like an iPhone 42?" Ray asked.

"Actually, yes," Older Ray said. "That's exactly what it is."

"Whoa. Did you make this?" Ray said. "Please tell me that we're some kind of brilliant, genius inventor!"

"Well . . . sort of! I helped on it," he said. "The foundational design was actually based on Joanna's later version of FuRo."

Viv's eyebrow raised at the mention of Joanna's name.

Wow. So Joanna did come back to work here, even after everything she did.

Ray turned the device over a few times in his hand. There were no buttons. No cameras. No visible features at all. He tapped at it a few times, but the screen wouldn't respond.

"Um, what does it do?" Ray asked.

Older Ray patted him on the shoulder. "The real question is what *doesn't* it do!"

He reached out and gave the device a series of rhythmic taps. In the blink of an eye, a spout of burning flames shot out of the bottom end of the phone.

"WHOA!" Ray said. "And you use this thing to make telephone calls?!"

Older Ray nodded with a wide grin.

"Are you going to teach me how to work it?" Ray asked.

The slight beeping noise from behind Older Viv's ear kicked up again.

"There's no time," she said.

Ray tucked the device into his shirt pocket, stirring the little alien that was curled up inside.

"Aw, baby Meekee!" Older Ray said.

The green ball of fluff peeked up from the pocket. When he saw the two Rays standing side by side, Meekee did a double take. He leapt into Older Ray's arms.

"I forgot how cute he looked when he was young!" The two nuzzled like cozy kittens.

"Wait, what does he look like now?" Ray asked.

Older Ray cupped his hands around Meekee's ears.

"Trust me. You don't wanna know."

Viv had patiently been waiting her turn, wondering when her amazing upgrade would be revealed, but the older Viv shut the drawer.

"Uh, is there a new combat suit?" Viv asked.

Older Viv spun on her heels.

"You won't need it," she said.

"What?"

"There's something else you need, but it's something that I can't show you," the new director said.

Oh, this should be good.

"What is it?" Viv asked.

"It's not here at the base," she said. "But we'll worry about that later. Right now we have two minutes to talk, so everybody make it fast."

With a nod, the older counterparts motioned for their younger selves to follow. Viv stayed with Older Viv as the others fanned out across the hall, giving each pairing some room for privacy.

It was quiet for a moment as the older Vivian fidgeted by the control table, her back turned to her younger self. Viv agonized over what to say. She rubbed at the back of her neck, hoping that a conversation topic would magically appear.

"Has anyone ever told you that you look just like Mom?" she said.

"Oh, all the time. Especially people here at the base," Older Viv said. "Want in on a little secret?"

The younger Viv nodded, hoping for a clue about the ring she'd seen earlier. Instead, the adult Vivian pulled at the lock of hair draped over her forehead.

"This strip of gray? It's totally fake."

"No. Really?"

"Yep. Mom's is, too. A little Harlow family secret."

"You're kidding me."

"I wish I was kidding. She says it makes people take you more seriously. She even ran a few studies on it."

Viv couldn't help but chuckle. "I had no idea."

The two shared a smile until Viv glanced down at Older Viv's hands, particularly the fourth finger on her left hand.

The ring was gone.

"You took off the wedding ring?" Viv asked.

"I'm sorry about that," Older Viv replied with a drawn-out sigh. "It really was a mistake. You weren't supposed to see it. We said we'd keep our personal lives a secret. Just like they did for us."

"Come on," the younger version pressed. "You can tell me. I mean, it's not like you'll be spoiling any surprise. It's gonna happen eventually."

"That's the thing. We don't know if it will happen eventually. Nothing is certain. Any information that you bring back to the past could easily alter our future, especially something as delicate and tricky as a relationship."

"Please? Pretty please? Just tell me who it is. A hint!" Viv begged.

"Be reasonable. Imagine if you went back knowing exactly who I was married to. It would completely change the way you interact with them!" Older Viv said.

"I could play it cool! Pretend that nothing's changed!" the younger Viv said.

"Oh yeah? Could you actually, though?"

". . . No."

"That's what I thought. Because at your age, I know that I wouldn't have been able to play it cool, either. The relationship has to progress naturally. Your future needs to be your own. But for what it's worth, I'm very happy with the way my life is. I wouldn't want anything to change."

The younger Viv twisted a lock of hair in her fingers, the tress right above her left eye. Someday destined to be gray, apparently.

All of a sudden, she felt a wave of melancholy hit her like a ton of bricks, almost as though her entire life had already been predetermined for her.

The older Viv gave a soft smile and knelt down on one knee. She wrapped Viv in her arms and squeezed tight, right between her shoulder blades. It was the same kind of hug her mom always gave.

"Come here," she said. "I want to show you something."

The older Viv opened up a drawer in the center console, pulling out a colorful box.

A puzzle?

She dumped it out onto the table, scattering the mismatched jigsaw pieces in an untidy pile.

"Watch this," she said.

The younger Viv took a few steps back and watched as the future version of herself took a deep breath. Older Viv focused her eyes and in an instant, they lit up with a fierce shade of green. The pieces floated up into the air and rearranged themselves, aligning into a perfect, completed puzzle within a matter of seconds. Using only her mind, she laid the puzzle gently back down flat on the table. Finally put together, the jigsaw turned out to be a picture of puppies in a basket. Viv was beyond impressed.

"How the heck did you do that?" she asked.

"Lots of practice," Older Viv said, her eyes returning to their normal shade of muted olive.

"That was, like, a thousand pieces!" the younger Viv said. "All I can seem to do is blow stuff up! And that's if I can even get my powers to work in the first place."

Older Viv smiled and patted her on the shoulder.

"Don't worry," she said. "Soon, you'll start to see that those powers you have—that *we* have—are a gift, not a curse."

A nearly imperceptible beeping sound quietly chirped from nearby. Older Viv tucked her hair behind her ear, revealing a tiny device floating dutifully just a few millimeters from her neck.

"It's exactly 3:11. Time for the next phase," she said.

"Next phase?" Viv asked.

Older Viv pressed two fingers to her lips and let out a sharp whistle, catching the attention of everyone in the room. She waved them back to the center console.

"And that's how I ended up with my bionic kidney!" Older Ray said, clearly just finishing up some kind of fantastical story. The younger Ray looked horrified.

"But what about that thing you were supposed to give me?" Viv asked as everybody gathered together again.

"Like I said, it's not here at the base. We'll have to teleport you," Older Viv replied.

"Teleport her?" Charlotte said.

"Yeah. It's actually quite simple. Nowadays, we use teleportation frequently here at the base," she explained. "We managed to cut down our carbon output. Cars and buses are practically obsolete. So if you were thinking about getting your driver's license, maybe hold off a little."

She pulled out a small, metallic disk and placed it on the floor, motioning for the younger Viv to step on. The teleportation pad was a simple platform made of smooth, silver metal, much more streamlined and simplified than the bulky time machine.

"Wow," Viv said. "That's all it takes?"

"Yep! This puppy right here could get you to Australia in a nanosecond," Older Charlotte said.

"Transgalactic travel, too," Older Elijah added.

"Transgalactic? You mean to other *planets*?" Viv asked.

"Other planets, other solar systems, even distant galaxies," Older Viv said. "And that's exactly where you'll be going."

Viv's eyes widened.

"Wait a second. You're sending me out of the solar system?" Viv asked.

"I volunteer! I wanna go!" Elijah said. "Dad always says the best pilots are the ones who make it to space."

"Sorry, pal, but this is a trip Viv has to make on her own," Older Charlotte said.

"On her own? You want to split us up?" Elijah said. "After everything we just went through? Nuh-uh. No way."

"I'm not leaving her, either," Charlotte said.

"Yeah! Me neither," Ray chimed in.

The adults all grinned from ear to ear.

"We said the exact same thing," the older Viv explained. "But I promise. She'll be fine."

The four kids traded a few concerned looks.

"Where are you sending me?" Viv asked.

"Planet ZR-18," Older Viv replied.

The name was instantly familiar

"Megdar's planet?" Viv asked. "You're sending me to the *Roswellian* planet?!"

"Oh, come on! I wanna go!" the younger Ray said.

"Only Viv can go. She's the only one capable of surviving in the Roswellian atmosphere," Older Viv explained.

"Yeah, you're right. Only Viv should go!" Ray recanted.

"You trust us, don't you?" Older Elijah said with a gleaming smile.

Viv nodded and took her place on the platform. Every eye in the room was glued to her.

"Keep the teleportation disk handy. It will light up when you're needed back on Earth," the older Viv instructed. "Are you ready?"

"Ready? Ready for what? I don't really know—"

"Find Megdar. He'll help you."

Older Viv slammed down on the button, and Viv's world turned to black.

CHAPTER
TWELVE

Wow. Older me was right. Teleportation is WAY better than time travel!

Viv's journey was so smooth that she felt like she was floating. In fact, she *was* floating. She stared down at her feet, but amazingly, there was no ground beneath her—just the teleportation plate hovering below her feet like a personal-pizza-size flying saucer. Whatever gravity held this planet together, the force seemed much weaker than Earth's. Viv peered past her legs, past her feet, all the way down into the glowing green interior and the core of the entire planet.

Whoa. What the heck?

All around her, the atmosphere wasn't blue. Instead, a deep purple hue filled the air. The clouds that floated by high in the sky were an electric green.

Is it even air?

Viv inhaled slowly, taking a deep breath into her lungs. The air felt thick—sort of what she imagined it might feel like to take a breath at the bottom of a jar of honey.

Iridescent bubbles floated by on the same breeze that mussed Viv's hair. And it wasn't just the bubbles. Everything was floating, suspended in some sort of buoyant gas. To her left, a hovering alien jungle loomed large in the sky. But they weren't plants. There were no leaves. No wood. Instead, they were towers of hovering organic formations, almost like the same rubbery flesh one might see on a mushroom. Their bumpy limbs stretched out and swayed in the gentle wind. Small creatures of all shapes and sizes hovered around the pillars—appendages, fins, antennae, and tentacles stuck out from every which direction. They glowed green in a rhythmic unison, as if tapped into some kind of internal heartbeat of the planet.

Out of nowhere, a flock of creatures that looked identical to Meekee swirled and danced through the air. They swept a few inches past Viv's head giggling the same high-pitched trill as Meekee.

Viv couldn't help but marvel at the tranquility of it all. An entire ecosystem of creatures living in perfect harmony.

It's paradise on earth.

Well, I guess not on Earth.

Viv craned her head back and looked toward the sky. Instead of a singular, powerful star serving as their sun, the sky was dotted with thousands of smaller, dimmer stars, and a thousand orbiting moons.

Then in an instant, the darkness fell on her like a heavy blanket. Something had blotted out the light coming from all those little stars and moons: something gigantic. Viv squinted up. It took her a moment to realize what she was looking at.

Whoa.

The creature was massive, practically the size of a football field. It had a biforked tail like a whale that it used to propel itself as it soared overhead. Trailing the colossal beast was a group of smaller creatures, riding on the air tunnel the huge alien whale had left in its wake.

Then Viv noticed the people . . . Well, not human people, but the Roswellians—the same kind of green, tentacled alien creatures she had fought off at the base. And they were staring right at her.

Well, it was a little difficult to tell exactly where they were staring, given their thousands of eyes. But one thing was for certain: They definitely noticed her.

Viv kicked at the air, but without much friction, it was difficult to steer in the direction she wanted. She floated along in a hapless path, catching a glimpse of herself in a passing bubble. She could feel her eyes glowing green, thrumming in the same cadence as the whole landscape.

Something rested gently on her shoulder.

"Ah!" Viv spun around with a fright, half expecting to end up inside the belly of some giant extraterrestrial shark.

But it was a Roswellian, a smaller one than those she was used to.

The Roswellian pointed a tentacle in Viv's direction, the alien's thousands of eyes lighting up with the reflected light of the nearby moons.

"Inaeiparpegklqnxbmerepiefnsogn?" the creature said, gurgling out the syllables like a blender filled with gravel.

"I'm sorry . . . I don't speak, umm . . ." Viv tried to convey ignorance with her body, but the sound of her foreign tongue was enough to send the frightened Roswellian scrambling. The alien floated off toward the rest of the group beyond the tallest pillar.

"Vivian?"

The voice nearly made Viv jump out of her skin. She tried to spin around, but the empty atmosphere made it tough to control her body. Nevertheless, she recognized the voice instantly.

"Megdar?" she said.

The alien leader looked almost nothing like he had back on Earth. Just a week earlier in Viv's timeline, he and Viv had fought each other in a heated battle in the Area 51 terrarium. Megdar had been consumed with enacting revenge for all the Roswellians being imprisoned at the base for so long . . . and for Viv's mother stealing his DNA for her own use.

The Roswellian leader floated around to face her. He looked better than he had on Earth. Stronger. Bigger. Healthier.

He was so fierce last week. But now . . . he seems so . . . gentle.

"Vivian," he said warmly. "You made it. Welcome to Mxjun-zinqoraboruzosnjurgioqlanambygxberuwetgedfnaoifnjdbkiez. Our home."

The sound of Megdar's Roswellian pronunciation made Viv's head hurt.

"Say that one more time, please?" Viv asked.

Megdar let out a hearty laugh. "Don't worry. The so-called Roswellian tongue is rather difficult for humans to master. You seem to be getting pretty good at it, though. Your future self, that is."

"Really?" Viv said. "Does she come here often?"

"Every now and then. She visited me here not too long ago. Told me that you'd be coming. Did she 'accidentally' show you her wedding ring?" Megdar said with a chuckle.

Viv blinked. "Yes? How did you know about that?"

"Whoops. Forget I said anything," Megdar replied, a bit of earnest embarrassment in his voice.

Whoa. The mistake of showing me the ring wasn't a mistake, either?

"But yes," Megdar said, trying to move the conversation along. "The Vivian I know comes here from time to time. Those teleportation pads certainly make it a whole lot easier. Anyway, we have much to discuss."

"Shouldn't we . . . go someplace else to talk? Somewhere private?" Viv asked.

"Oh no, it's all right. Only a few citizens on this planet speak English. Those of us who were unlucky enough to be on that spaceship all those years ago. Trust me, no one understands a word we're saying. Also, I could turn into my human form if you'd like. Happy to do anything that might make you feel more comfortable," Megdar offered.

"No, that's okay," Viv said. "This place is surprisingly . . . relaxing."

"You know, this is the place I wanted to take you all those years ago. Well, I suppose for you, it was about a week ago."

"It's beautiful. I see why you wanted to get back so badly. We don't have anything like this on Earth."

"Many of your people believe that Earth is the only planet with life at all," Megdar said.

"Well, that's because most people don't even know aliens exist. How have you managed to stay hidden for so long?" Viv said.

"Vivian, we haven't been hiding. In fact, quite the opposite. Our people have friends all across the galaxy. We have relationships with numerous intelligent species in the universe. I even have a vacation house on COCONUTS-2b," Megdar explained.

"Oh, come on. That's not a real planet," Viv said.

"Well, that's the name your people have for it, but yes it is!" he said. "A lovely gas giant about six times larger than your Jupiter."

"Sounds . . . nice?"

Megdar let out a sigh. "Yes, it is. But of all the planets I've traveled to, only one has attacked my people and held us hostage for more than fifty years."

Viv shuffled her feet against the nonexistent ground. "Was it . . . the Martians?"

"Very funny," Megdar said.

"Not really a good look for humanity, is it?" Viv said.

Not a good look for her mother, either. Her mom hadn't been the one to initially mistreat the Roswellians, but she hadn't exactly let them go after she took over as director, either. Part of Viv knew her mom kept some secrets to protect her, but she still wished she'd let down a few walls now and then.

"Don't blame yourself. Compared to our species, yours is a relatively primitive society. You've got a few millions of years before you really get your act together."

The teleportation disk threatened to float away. Megdar reached out one of his lengthy tentacles and pulled the device back toward Viv. She wrapped her arms around it and held tight.

"I understand that you're trying to find your father," Megdar continued. "Is that right?"

"Yeah. He's been missing for a while, now," Viv said.

"You know, I met your father once," Megdar replied.

"Really? You probably know him better than I do," Viv said.

"I snapped his arm like a twig," Megdar admitted.

"You *what*?"

"I didn't mean to hurt him. It was completely by accident. And it happened a long, long time ago—back when we were being held as captives, when your scientists were trying to get my DNA. For a moment, I let my anger get the best of me."

Viv bit the inside of her lip. The pain of his imprisonment, even after all this time, clearly still haunted Megdar.

"I'm sorry they did that to you," Viv said.

"You know, I used to be so angry about it. But with more time that has passed, the memories still hurt, but my need for revenge stings less and less. And knowing that it all led to you, I suppose it all worked out for the best," Megdar explained. "Now, all we need to do is get you in control of your powers."

Viv felt the hair on the back of her neck stand up.

"You can teach me about my powers?" she said, feeling a burst of hope swelling inside her.

Mom might not want me to use my powers . . . but if I could control them, maybe she'll feel differently.

"Of course," Megdar said. "Here on this planet, we don't really consider them powers at all. It's more like the way you can blink or breathe. It's part of you. Your DNA. It lies deep within you. It's a part of every nucleus of every cell in your body. It's not something you learn."

"I don't understand," Viv said.

"You're the first of your kind, Vivian," he said. "There's not much we know about you. We don't know how powerful you'll become. Or even how long you'll live. We Roswellians have merged DNA with many species in this galaxy. But never humankind. You're the progeny, Vivian. It's important to me that you carry on the positive legacy of our species.

"Let's start with that." He motioned to the gargantuan organic formation. In its entirety, it was nearly the size of a skyscraper.

"Now, I want you to lift that jungle."

"What? I can't do that!" Viv said. "You should've seen me earlier. I could barely pick up a bone off the ground!"

"Just try it," he said. "Focus. Feel your powers. Channel that deeper part of yourself."

Viv took a deep breath, trying to clear her mind of everything: the pirates. The apes. The numerous close encounters with death. Everything. She extended her arm out into the air, pointing her palm straight toward her target.

She strained hard. The veins in her forehead were beginning to bulge out. But nothing. Sweat began to build up along her hairline.

Come on, powers! We can do this!

She flexed every muscle in her body, feeling the boiling of her powers prickling beneath every inch of her skin. But it was no use.

Viv lowered her arm with a huff. "Nothing happened!"

"Exactly," Megdar said. "And why did nothing happen?"

Viv threw her arms up into the air,

"I don't know!" Viv said. "Isn't that what you're supposed to tell me?"

"It's not moving because you don't *care* if it moves or not," Megdar said.

"What do you mean? Of course, I care!" Viv defended.

"But do you really? Do you really care if that jungle lifts up a few inches? For my species, our powers are controlled by something we call *gaenfouaureoqnagesrpt*. But in terms of humanity, I suppose you could translate it to *desires of the soul*."

"Desires of the soul? What the heck is that supposed to mean? Sounds like the kind of book my mom would read."

"It means that your powers will only kick in when it's something you really, truly want. The power will come from deep inside you. But your desires and your emotions must be in tune with one another. Achieve that, and you won't even need to think about it. It will come naturally."

"But I just saw my older self piece together a puzzle," Viv said. "You're telling me that putting that puzzle together was a desire of her soul?"

"That's just the thing. In your older years, you've learned how to become completely in tune with your gaenfouaureoqnagesrpt. You've found a way to care about everything," Megdar explained.

"But sometimes my powers explode out of me and I can barely control them," Viv said, thinking back to her battle in the desert against the Chupacabra. "And other times, I can't use my powers at all. Even when I do care. Even in the last day or so, my powers have felt weaker than they ever have."

"Yes, when your desires and emotions are not in harmony, your powers can be unwieldy," Medgar said. "I'm assuming those moments when you felt overwhelmed by your abilities were times when you were similarly overwhelmed by your emotions?"

Viv considered it for a moment before nodding.

"There you go! Physical or mental exhaustion can also lead to a deficiency in your powers," Megdar said. "Our species requires no sleep, so I theorize it's your human side that causes these deficiencies."

Of course. That explains why they've been so unreliable lately.

"But there's nothing stopping you from overcoming these deficiencies. Imagine it this way: If you tried to lift weights after not sleeping for twenty-four hours, it would probably be a lot harder than if you were well rested. But with a disciplined focus and control over your emotions and your desires, it is possible."

The teleportation disk in Viv's hand suddenly zapped to life, lighting up with a mesmerizing chrome glow.

"It's time," Megdar said. "They're calling you back."

"Right now? But I'm not ready! I have more questions!" Viv cried out.

Megdar curled his tentacle gently around her shoulder.

"She said you might say that," he stated. "There's nothing to fear. Just stay in control of your gaenfouaureoqnagesrpt, and everything will be okay."

"No!" Viv protested. "You can't send me back like this!"

The transportation disk burned red-hot in her hands.

"Have a little more trust in yourself, Viv," he said. "You have the power of the entire Roswellian people behind you. I believe in you. We believe in you. Now, go. The people of Earth need you."

Using his telekinetic powers, Megdar placed Viv onto the floating transportation disk.

"Please! Just a little longer!" Viv said.

"Go!" Megdar instructed. "Before it's too late!"

The sparkling platform activated, shooting a beam of light straight up through the thick, purple atmosphere.

And just like that, Viv teleported out of sight.

CHAPTER THIRTEEN

By the time Viv returned to the year 2050, the Continuum Navigation wing had fallen deadly silent. She expected a hero's welcome, having just completed her first intergalactic trip and even more impressively, making it back in one piece.

But instead, her three friends barely noticed her. They were gathered with their adult counterparts, hovered around a camera feed from a holographic screen near the front of the room. A few seconds passed before the older Viv glanced over her shoulder, noticing the younger girl who had just miraculously transported across countless galaxies in the blink of eye.

"Good. You're back," Older Viv said.

"What's happening?" Viv asked. "Why'd you call me back?"

"The base's security system picked up a signal. There's some unusual chronometric activity gathering outside the compound."

"What does that mean?" Viv asked.

"They've arrived. They're closing in on the base," Older Viv replied.

"Who's 'they'?" Viv asked. "What's going on?"

"It's those scary robe guys, isn't it? The man with the sand hand?" Ray said, holding Meekee tight to his chest.

Older Viv pressed at the tiny device floating by her ear, projecting another hologram out into the room. It was a live-feed camera, and it showed a terrifying sight. Circling the cloaking system that surrounded the base, a tornado of sand was building. It cast a dark, gritty shadow over the entirety of Area 51.

"Director Harlow?" a voice from the projection said. "We're stationed at the western checkpoint, but it's looking pretty bad out here."

"Hold your ground," she said. "They're coming this way. The cloaking device will hold for a little while, but it won't last forever."

"Those sand guys who were chasing us . . . what *are* they?" Elijah asked.

Older Viv sighed and scratched at her temples. "We think they might be ancient entities. Physical manifestations of time itself. But that's just our best guess. For years we've been trying to find any record of them, any information in the universe about their existence, but it seems that they're rather elusive . . . and quite possibly dangerous."

"From observing their behavior, we believe their goal is to eliminate anyone who's not in their proper timeline," Older Elijah said.

"And considering the fact that there's no record of them anywhere throughout history, it seems like they're pretty good at their jobs," Older Charlotte said.

Yikes.

"The Nicks of Time," the older Ray added. "Or at least that's what we've been calling them."

The Nicks of Time?

"They're the reason Dad can't stay in one place for too long," Older Viv said. "Somehow, they can lock onto a time signature. He got stuck in that time loop all those years ago because of them, and they've been chasing him ever since. Trying to eliminate him from the chronological plane itself."

"So . . . that's why he couldn't come back?" Viv said. Older Viv gave her a solemn nod.

"Why do you call them the Nicks of Time?" the younger Ray asked.

The adults gave a collective shrug.

"The name just kind of stuck," Older Elijah said.

"And, if you ask me, they all look like their names could be Nick," Older Ray added.

"It's funny you say that. I was thinking Mick," Ray said. "But Nick is much better."

"If memory serves, you kids have already encountered the three of them," Older Viv said. "You were lucky to make it out alive. If they manage to touch you, they'll turn you into sand—completely erasing you and any trace of you from the history of the universe."

"Geez," Ray chimed in. "That seems pretty harsh."

"Nobody will remember that you ever existed. Not your teachers. Not your parents. Not even one another."

"Like that time you forgot to invite me to your birthday party, Elijah," the younger Ray said. "Remember that?"

"Right. Just like that . . . ," Elijah said.

"That's why you guys need to get out of here," Older Viv added.

"That's nice of you guys to look out for us like that," Ray said.

"You doofus," Charlotte said. "We're them! If we get erased, they get erased!"

"It's true. If any of those three robe-wearing weirdos touch you, we'll cease to exist, too," Older Elijah explained.

Older Viv bent down and wrapped the younger Viv with a hug, whispering into her ear.

"Your next stop is December 17, 1905," she said. "Type those coordinates into the machine, and you'll find your next clue. You'll be one step closer to finding Dad."

"You're sure? You guys calculated for daylight saving time?" Viv asked.

"Yes, I'm sure," she said with a chuckle. "Head there and don't come back. You guys can do this."

She twisted the dials on the temporal transporter hanging around Viv's neck until it matched the right date.

"Are you sure you don't want us to stay and help?" Viv asked.

"We said the exact same thing when we were your age," Older Charlotte said. "Don't you worry about us. If the older versions of us could do it, we can, too. Besides, just because we're here now doesn't mean that you lot won't make different choices than we did and change the future for us. If you leave now, that's one less choice for us to have to worry about."

"It's time. Let's go, guys. You all need to get out of here."

Older Viv corralled the kids toward the bay of time machines.

"Can we take one of the ones that doesn't make you puke?" Ray asked.

"Sorry, buddy! It's gotta be the one you came in on!" the older Elijah said.

"Wait," Charlotte said. "Do you guys hear that?"

Everyone stopped moving.

At first, it was just a few grains pinging onto the floor. The microscopic bits of sand seemed to materialize out of nowhere, just a couple of inches away from Elijah's face. He took a few wobbling steps backward, nearly knocking over his older self.

All of a sudden, the few grains of sand had morphed into a steady stream, spilling out onto the floor in a weighty heap. The stream turned into a vortex of sand, swirling into a full-blown tornado.

"They're here. You gotta go! NOW!" Older Viv commanded. She pushed the kids into the beaten, misshapen time machine they'd arrived in.

"We'll hold them off!" Older Charlotte said. She pulled out a horseshoe-shaped gadget and circled the quickly rising mass of sand.

"Remember the next coordinates I told you!" Older Viv instructed.

And with that, the doors to the time machine slammed shut.

"Guys?" Ray asked. "What happens if the older version of me gets turned into sand?"

"Guess you'll disappear, Ray," Charlotte said. "We'll miss you, buddy."

"You won't even remember me!" Ray cried.

"Enough, guys! We gotta go!" Elijah said.

"I got the controls!" Ray said, sliding in front of the control panel. "Older me said our next stop is December 17, 1490!"

"No, it's December 17, 1903!" Elijah said. "I'm sure of it!"

"You guys are all crazy! Older me said it was December 17, 1808!" Charlotte said.

"But look! Older Ray already put the coordinates in on my temporal transporter!" Ray said.

"Well, he was wrong, because Older Charlotte put in my date! See?" Charlotte said.

Uh-oh. That's not good.

"Should we open the door and double-check?" Ray asked.

An explosion rocked the time machine, sending bits of sand raining down from the cracks in the ceiling.

"I think that's a no!" Charlotte said.

"Viv?" Elijah said. "Any clue which one is right?"

"Older me said December 17, 1905," she said.

"Well, that's close enough to mine!" Elijah said. "Let's split the difference and call it 1904!"

"Guys, I really think it was 1490!" Ray said.

"No!" Charlotte said. "It's gotta be 1808! Enough arguing! Let's get out of here!"

With a swift bump of her hip, Charlotte nudged Ray away from the control panel and began furiously scrolling through the coordinates. Then Elijah came swooping in. Ray reached into the fray. The dial on the time machine's dashboard spun wildly.

"Stop!" Viv said. "Calm down!"

But it was no use. The panic had already gripped her friends. Viv stuck her arm in, trying to pry everyone away from the controls, but only succeeding in accidentally messing with the dial herself.

The rocking and quaking happening outside only added to the confusion and chaos. Sparks of electricity flew through the air. The time machine crackled, buzzed, and sputtered.

"It's going haywire!" Viv shouted. "Everybody, hold on!"

Viv snatched Ray's hand and held tight. With her other hand, she grabbed Elijah and pulled him close. The kids all squeezed one another in a tight hug. Meekee was compressed in the middle of them all, struggling to catch his breath.

ZAP! ZAP! ZAP! ZAP!

The fabric of the time portal split open with a loud, ripping screech. But this wasn't like any of the other portals before.

This time, there were *four*.

She felt her grip on Ray's hand slip away. Elijah's was next. One by one, she watched as the faces of her friends were stretched and distorted, rapidly pulled into each of the swirling time portals until finally, Viv felt her own body atomize into the ether.

CHAPTER FOURTEEN

The throbbing in Elijah's head was almost unbearable. Every cell of his insides felt like they'd been twisted into knots. Somehow, after the frenzied portals opened, he'd landed face-down in the sand. He scrambled to his feet the second he managed to pry his eyes open.

"Guys?" he said out loud to no one. The time machine was nowhere to be seen. Just an endless stretch of sand and dunes. He was utterly alone.

He bent down and scooped up a palmful of sand, letting the grains run through his open fingers. A freezing cold wind whipped up off the dunes and stung at his eyes.

No! Those robed guys! They got me! I'm lost in the sands of time! We broke the time machine.

He balled up his fists at his sides and fought off the urge to scream.

"Hello? Is anybody there?" His voice crackled under the emotion threatening to seep through. It was the first time he'd been alone since Joanna had left him stranded in the tundra within Area 51, freezing and afraid. That eerie feeling that something bad was about to happen crept in yet again.

This is no time to panic. Keep your cool.

He took a few careful steps forward. At least the ground beneath his feet felt sturdy. Though he wouldn't be surprised if he stepped into an endless pit. The wind swept across the sands and stung his eyes. Elijah managed a few more steps before a rumbling sound sent him diving back down toward the sand.

What the heck is that?

The sound was tinny, almost mechanical. Elijah covered his head, convinced that some giant grandfather clock monster was about to appear. But as quickly as it began, the sound abruptly stopped. It was soon replaced with the faint hint of a voice—a human voice.

Someone's here! Maybe I'm not lost in the sands of time after all!

Elijah followed the sound, his trail of footprints being eerily erased in the sand behind him with each gust of wind. He scurried up one of the dunes and rubbed at his eyes to make sure what he was seeing wasn't a hallucination.

At the bottom of the dune, two finely dressed men stood around a makeshift airplane. They gestured wildly to each other, and Elijah was finally able to make out what they were saying.

"Well done, old chap!" one of the men said. "You've fouled the propeller yet again!"

"I implore you. It is surely a problem with the motor," the other man replied.

"I checked the motor this morning! It was working just fine!" the first man said. "It simply must be the propeller."

They argued over what seemed to be a primitive aircraft, fit with a long canard wing configuration, twin propellers, and a small gasoline-powered engine. The men were skinny, with long, slender faces to match. The taller one had a prominent bald spot circling the top of his scalp. The other had a thick, demonstrative mustache perched on his upper lip.

Do I go down there? I don't think I'll be able to get out of here by myself . . . But everybody said I shouldn't interfere with the timeline! What do I do?!

Elijah watched the men cautiously from on top of the ridge. The two figures moved around the aircraft, furiously adjusting hinges and screws, arguing all the while.

Ugh, I can't just wait up here forever! Plus, how much harm can I really do?

With a deep breath, he took his first step down the dune. He cleared his throat and hoped a friendly tone would convey that he meant no harm.

"Nice machine you've got there!" Elijah said.

The two men jumped nearly a foot in the air when they heard Elijah's voice.

"What on earth? You've almost given us heart attacks, dear boy! Who in the world are you?" the man with the heavy mustache asked.

"I'm so sorry to interrupt," he said. "My name is Elijah, and I think I might be lost."

"I'll say!" the shorter man said. "How did you manage to find yourself all the way out here?"

"Where exactly is here?" Elijah asked.

The men each raised a curious brow.

"Have you hit your head? You're in Kill Devil Hills, my boy," one of the men said.

Elijah gulped down a wad of spit.

"Kill . . . Devil Hills? You're not going to hurt me, are you?" he asked.

"Hurt you?" the man said with a laugh. "Oh no! Certainly not! It is quite a scary name, is it not? I much prefer Kitty Hawk."

Kitty Hawk?

Those two words set off an alarm bell in Elijah's head.

The plane. The two men.

"Excuse me . . . by any chance, are you two the Wright brothers?" he asked.

The two men looked at him with an incredulous glare.

"Yes, indeed we are. I'm Wilbur, and that's my brother, Orville," the bald man said.

"And how have you possibly gathered that information,

dear boy? Say, you aren't one of Sam Langley's men, are you? Sent here to spy on our progress?" Orville added.

"What? No! I don't even know who that is. I-I-I can't believe this! I'm standing in front of *the* Wright brothers! This is amazing! You two are legends!" Elijah said.

No way! They're the flipping founding fathers of aviation!

"I beg your pardon?" Orville said. "Sorry, but I'm not quite sure what you mean."

Elijah tried to hide the excitement in his voice, but a little bit squeaked out, anyway. "Wow! The Wright brothers. What an honor to meet you! I've heard all about you."

The brothers scoffed and shared a bristly chuckle. Wilbur nudged Orville in the side with an elbow.

"I suppose Mother has been rather braggadocious at her book club again," he said. "Nobody around here knows us."

Oh yeah. Crud. I'm supposed to be from 1903!

"Yes! Your mom, Mrs. Wright! That's where I know you from! You two are geniuses . . . from what I've heard!" said Elijah nervously.

"Well, that is quite a kind sentiment, but we're merely humble inventors, my boy," Orville added.

"So, this must be it, huh?" Elijah said, tapping his hand against the spruce wood frame. "The Wright Flyer—uh, I mean . . . your invention?"

Orville stroked at his mustache. "Flyer? Oh, how we wish it would. Regrettably, we've encountered quite a host of problems. The machine would undoubtedly have flown beautifully if not for the mechanical failures."

Elijah reached his hand into his pocket and felt at the tiny wondrous orb he'd just been given back at the base. He considered it for a moment, what it would be like to show these early-twentieth-century inventors something so technologically advanced—the pinnacle of man-made flight.

If only they knew . . .

"Maybe I could take a look at the plane for you," Elijah said. "I'm pretty good with this kind of thing."

"And what exactly do you know about flight, son?" Wilbur prodded.

"All sorts of things! My dad is in the Air Force. He taught me practically everything he knows," Elijah said.

The two brothers exchanged a puzzled look.

"The . . . Air Force?" Wilbur asked.

Oh yeah. Whoops. I guess that doesn't exist yet.

"Never mind," Elijah said. "You said you were having trouble with the motor?"

"The propellers," Orville said. Wilbur rolled his eyes.

"Do you mind if I give it a try?" Elijah said.

He grabbed onto one of the wings and wrapped his hands around the scaffolding. With one strong yank, he heaved himself onto the deck.

"Whoa! Be careful there, son! This aeroplane is a highly complicated and delicate piece of machinery!" Wilbur protested.

Elijah shimmied belly up onto the wing platform where the motor sat. Without a second thought, he rolled up his sleeves and got to work.

No . . . Not that . . . Not that . . .

"Ah," he said. "Here's the problem!"

Elijah reached into the motor and adjusted the position of an electrical switch.

"I found the issue. Your contact breaker wasn't set right. That's why you weren't getting a spark in your combustion chamber."

The two brothers watched his every move, pure amazement filling their eyes.

"Also, this should help, too," Elijah said. He cranked back on the pulley rope that controlled the hinged joints to the fabric wings. The entire wing lifted up a few degrees.

"For takeoff, you'll want this a little higher. It will help with the angle of attack. Especially in this wind. Trust me."

And with that, Elijah flipped on the engine. The motor roared to life, sending the two propellers spinning at a lively pace. Even without anyone piloting it yet, the flyer looked like it was ready to take off on its own.

The brothers stood with their mouths completely agape.

"Boy, you've done it! How on earth did you figure that out so quickly?" Orville exclaimed.

"Beginner's luck, I guess," Elijah said with a smile.

"What are we waiting for? Let's give her a try!" Wilbur

shouted over the sound of the engine. He helped Elijah down from the airframe and began to climb up into the pilot's position.

Orville laid a hand on Wilbur's shoulder.

"Oh no you don't, brother," Orville said. "You've had your chance. It's my turn now."

Wilbur frowned. "Fine, have it your way," he grunted. "But if this test proves to be a success, I'll never let you hear the end of it!"

Orville took his place lying belly down in the hip cradle, making sure the rudders and the corresponding wires were all functioning properly.

Wilbur led Elijah around to the back of the aeroplane. Orville adjusted his cap and gave a thumbs-up.

"Three, two, one! Now!" Wilbur shouted.

Elijah helped Wilbur shove the hefty aircraft beyond the launching rail. The flyer coasted down the dune, using gravity to its advantage, and then it took off, clearing a good twelve feet off the ground. Wilbur exploded with an array of joyous hoots and hollers. Orville and the primitive airplane managed to fly about the distance of a football field before landing softly in the sand.

Wilbur took off down the beach, running to catch up with his now airworthy brother. Smiling ear to ear, Elijah broke into a sprint after him.

Even though Elijah had seen thousands of takeoffs in

his lifetime, seeing this one was different.

It felt like seeing a miracle.

"You're an engineering genius, my boy!" Wilbur exclaimed. He lifted Elijah up off the sand and spun him around in joyful circles. Once the flyer was safely settled on the ground and the engine was switched off, Orville took a leaping jump off the wings to join in on the group hug.

"We've done it my boy! You've done it!" he exclaimed. The three took a moment to catch their breath and calm the adrenaline.

"Say, how would you like to come back to Dayton with us? We could offer you a job at our bicycle shop?" Wilbur asked.

"Bicycle shop?" Elijah said. "Believe me. After this, you two won't be working at a bicycle shop anymore."

"Say, son. Aren't you cold?" Orville said. "Here you are. Take my jacket." The mustached man slid his arms out from the sleeves. He extended the stiff collar of the overcoat toward Elijah's widening eyes.

"Oh no," Elijah said. "I couldn't. I can't take this! You just made history in this jacket!"

"Take it? I'm not giving it to you, boy," Orville said. "Just to borrow. Give it back to me next time we see each other."

"Right . . . ," Elijah said. He didn't see a way he could refuse without having to explain his whole situation, so he slid his arms into the sleeves. The coat itself was a bit big for

Elijah's thin frame, but the warmth of the wool felt comforting nonetheless.

"Honestly, this is the least we can do. Is there any other way we can repay you? We would've been out here until the next dawn had you not come along," Wilbur added.

"Actually . . . yes. There is. Two things in fact," Elijah said.

"Name them, and we'll see what we can do," Orville offered.

"First, I need you to promise you'll never tell anyone that I helped you with your plane."

The brothers looked confused. "Really? Are you certain?" Wilbur asked.

"Positive," Elijah said. The men exchanged a glance, shrugged, and then nodded.

"If you insist, I suppose we can take all the credit," Orville said. "What's the second thing?"

"I need help getting back to my friends."

CHAPTER FIFTEEN

"HELLOOOO?"

Charlotte's voice echoed against the vintage wood, rattling the fine china cabinets and nearly sending a row of glass figurines careening toward the ground.

"Very funny, Viv!" she shouted. "Come on. Seriously? Where are you guys?"

She'd woken up with her body wedged in the corner of a tight hallway. The floorboards creaked as she propped herself up.

"Ray? Elijah?" she said. "Meekee?"

A beam of moonlight poured in through one of the thick glass-paned windows. Wherever she was, the entire place had a strange musty smell, as if those windows hadn't been opened in weeks. The scent of burning oil lamps wafted down the hall.

What the heck happened back there? Where am I?

"Hello? Is there anybody here?" she said. "If any of you

weirdo robe guys are out there, you better show yourselves! I swear, I'll—"

Before she could finish her threat, a booming noise shook the entire building. It was unmistakable: the sound of a thundering piano.

"Blimey!" Charlotte shouted.

She stepped gently down the hall toward the music. Stacks of old, leatherbound books lined the walls. Each of the titles were written in a foreign language she couldn't understand. With every step she took farther into the building, the piano was getting louder and more discordant. Charlotte descended a wrought iron spiral staircase, grimacing at the horrible sound, like somebody was banging on the keys with closed fists.

As she gingerly stepped down the lower corridor, the sound suddenly stopped, plunging the entire building into silence. Charlotte gripped onto the wooden threshold of the doorway and peeked around the corner.

Holy smokes.

Set deep against the back wall of the messy room, a magnificent black piano shimmered beneath the light of several candles and lamps. A man, hunched with his back turned to her, sat on the bench in front of the keys.

Well, that's pretty scary.

Charlotte took a step to her left, hoping to get a better look at the man's face. Her hip bumped ever so gently into one of the display cabinets, sending a glass trophy tumbling off the shelf. It cracked down onto the floor and exploded into a million little pieces.

Crud. Crud. Crud.

Sure that she'd given herself away, Charlotte stood as still as a statue.

But the man didn't look back.

Huh?

She took a louder step with her foot, deliberately crunching some of the glass. Yet still no response from the mysterious piano man.

Can this guy hear anything at all?

"E-excuse me?" Charlotte asked.

But still, the man didn't notice.

"Hello? Sir?" she tried again.

Still nothing.

"Are you really there, or am I imagining all of this?" Charlotte said aloud. "Hey, mister! I'm talking to you!"

With a swift flick of his wrist, the man resumed banging on the keys. The sound was so loud and chaotic, Charlotte had to plug her ears.

"Geez! Could you play a little softer? I can't even hear myself think!" Her patience beginning to wear thin, Charlotte marched up to the piano bench and tapped the man on the shoulder. He leapt up from his seat with a fright.

A pair of deep brown, piercing eyes sat below his broad

forehead. The man sported a thicket of wavy brown hair atop his head. His collar rose up to his neck, giving him an almost turtlelike appearance.

"Wer bist du?!" the man shouted.

"What?" Charlotte replied.

"Wer bist du?! Wie bist du hierher gekommen?!" The man's language was harsh and choppy.

Charlotte shook her head in confusion.

"Sprechen Sie Deutsch?" he practically shouted.

"Huh?" Charlotte replied.

The man shook his head and threw his exasperated arms up in a huff.

"Français?" he shouted.

"Do I speak French? No?" Charlotte shouted back.

"Wer bist du?" the man said, pointing an accusatory finger in Charlotte's direction.

"Huh?" Charlotte said.

"Wer bist du?!" His temper flared.

"I'm sorry, but I don't understand. I'm just looking for my friends. Have you seen three tired-looking kids and a tiny green alien?"

"Ich kann dich nicht hören!" he shouted, pointing toward his ears.

"I DON'T KNOW WHAT YOU'RE SAYING!" Charlotte yelled.

"Geh weg! Ich habe in fünf Tagen ein Konzert im Theater

an der Wien!" His voice was loud. Nearly just as booming as the piano. Though the words sounded foreign, one stuck out in Charlotte's ears.

"Konzert? You have a concert?" Charlotte said in return.

The man spun back around to the piano, somehow even more frustrated than he had been a few moments ago. He returned to his "playing," little more than the kind of banging on the keys you could expect from a toddler. Charlotte's eyes scanned the music rack. Page after page of musical notation all had the same chicken-scratch signature in the bottom corner: LVB.

Wait a second. No way . . . No way!

"LUDWIG? LUDWIG VAN BEETHOVEN?" Charlotte shouted.

For a moment, the man stopped his mad pawing. He gave her an inquisitive look.

"Is this you? Are you LVB? Ludwig van Beethoven?" Charlotte asked, tapping her finger on the signature in the corner of the page.

"Ja?" he said, nodding. "Das bin ich."

Charlotte slapped her hands down onto his shoulders and shook him with excitement.

"I KNEW it!" she said. "Crikey, this is so cool!"

Beethoven shoved her off and away from his personal space, but Charlotte was completely unperturbed. She knew she should be trying to get back to her friends and not interacting with one of the greatest composers in history, but she couldn't resist perching at the edge of the piano like a starstruck fangirl.

"So whatcha working on? Which incredible magnum opus do you have in the pipeline?" she asked with a smile. She gestured toward the piano. "Let's hear what you've got!"

Beethoven cracked his neck in both directions. He placed his hands down on the keys, let out an exhausted gust of breath. His fingers stumbled over the keys. There was no discernible rhythm, no melody nor harmonies that tied the piece together—just a heavy brick wall of sound. Finally, mercifully, after a few minutes, even he seemed to be sick of the sound. He stopped playing and looked up at Charlotte. His mouth melted into a disappointed scowl.

"That's um . . . Wow," Charlotte said. She gave him a half-hearted thumbs-up. "That's really something."

What the heck? I thought this guy was supposed to be a musical genius or something.

Beethoven let out a pained grunt and ran his fingers through his hair like he was trying to rip some out. He collapsed facedown onto the piano. The keys rang out with a cacophonous swell, as if his frustration was speaking for itself.

"Writer's block, huh?" Charlotte said. "I get that too sometimes."

Ludwig was distraught, tearing up pages of sheet music

and scattering the strips all over the ivories.

Charlotte took a quick glance around the room. In the back of her head, Charlotte knew that it probably wasn't the best idea to be interacting with Beethoven this way, because of the timeline and not affecting the future and blah blah blah. But she couldn't stand to see this great man struggling this way.

Hmm . . . How can I communicate with him?

In the corner of the room, a pile of neglected instruments gathered dust. She squinted through the darkness. A familiar shape caught her eye. Nestled under an old harpsichord, propped up against a broken-stringed mandolin, a perfectly intact guitar practically called her name.

"Yes!" she said, picking up the old instrument and dusting it off. She plucked at the strings. The notes were in complete disarray. "Geez, ever heard of tuning your instruments?"

Beethoven didn't move an inch.

Guess not.

Charlotte fiddled with the tuning pegs for a while, plucking at the strings until the six notes sounded perfectly in line. After a few strums getting acquainted with the fretboard and the old steel strings, she felt ready to perform. She tapped on Beethoven's shoulder. The man lifted his head in sorrow.

DUN DUN DUN DUNN
DUN DUN DUN DUNNNNN

The notes rang out from the old guitar with as much ferocity as Charlotte could muster.

Beethoven's eyes widened in amazement. He jumped up from the piano and pressed his face up against the body of the guitar.

"Whoa! Easy there, Ludwig! What are you doing?" Charlotte asked.

"Wieder!" Beethoven commanded. He spun his finger around in a circular motion. "Wieder! Wieder! Wieder!"

"You want me to play it again?" she asked.

"Ja! Ja!" Beethoven shouted with his cheek scrunched up against the instrument.

"Well, okay!"

DUN DUN DUN DUNN!

DUN DUN DUN DUNNNNN!

The vibrations shook the guitar's wooden frame. Beethoven's face melted into the music. His entire demeanor changed, like somebody had given him a brain massage. He rushed back to his piano, swiping the sheet music filled with musical ramblings to the floor. He grabbed an inkwell, a feather quill, and went to work transposing the notes onto the page.

He took another deep breath and then let it rip.

DUN DUN DUN DUNNNN

DUN DUN DUN DUNNNNNN

The sound was electric—infinitely fuller and more

commanding than what a few strings on a guitar were capable of.

"Hey! There ya go!" she said. "Now you're sounding like the Beethoven I know!"

He twisted around on his piano bench. The rest of the symphony came flowing out of his fingertips. He smiled as he played. In place of the grimace that seemed to be concretely melted onto his face, a stream of tears flowed from his eyes.

"Oh come on, Ludwig! No need to get so emotional!" Charlotte said.

Once he made it halfway through the first movement, he scooped her up in his arms and twirled her around.

"Danke!" he said. "Danke! Danke! Danke, du kleines seltsames Kind."

"Don't thank me! You're the one who wrote it!" Charlotte said.

Beethoven went back to the keys and picked up where he left off.

"Ludwig. I know we just met, but I feel like I can trust you," Charlotte said over the sound of the music. "You haven't happened to see any time machines around here, have you?"

Beethoven shook his head and pointed at his ears.

"TIME MACHINE?" Charlotte said louder. "DO YOU HAVE ANY TIME MACHINES AROUND HERE?"

Beethoven shook his head and turned back to the expanse

of black-and-white keys that made him so happy. He contin
ued playing, completely unfazed by Charlotte's presence, lost
once again in the music.

"Ugh. It's hopeless," Charlotte said, plopping down on the
floor.

Well, great. Now how do I get out of here?

CHAPTER SIXTEEN

Of all the places the time portal could have spit him out, Ray landed facedown in a pile of manure. Meekee jumped onto the back of his head and tried desperately to wake him from his stupor. Finally, the unbearable stench tickled Ray's nose enough to force his eyes open.

"Oh come on!" Ray cried, picking himself up from the muck. He took a few wobbly steps to the side and peeled off his now-stained shirt.

The smell of the fertilizer mixed with the motion sickness from that last time jump made Ray throw up. Unfortunately, he threw up on top of the manure, creating an even worse mixture. Even Meekee looked queasy.

With so much of his puke now spanning hundreds of years across the timeline, Ray wondered if he had maybe set some kind of world record.

"Yeah, yeah, Charlotte," Ray said. "Sorry I 'pulled a Ray,' you guys—"

But when the ridicule didn't come, Ray suddenly realised he was completely alone.

"Hello?" His voice shook. "Is anybody there?"

Viv, Elijah, and Charlotte were nowhere to be seen. And there wasn't any trace of the time machine, either.

Uh-oh. That's not good.

"Guess it's just us, buddy," Ray said.

"Meekee! Ray! Ray and Meekee!" the tiny alien said in return. It was times like these that Ray was glad he'd adopted a super-powerful extraterrestrial alien to be his best friend.

Ray tucked Meekee into his pocket and surveyed his surroundings. He was in a medieval town square. The buildings were all made of red brick, and he could see the spires of a cathedral poking out beyond the skyline. In fact, the entire area looked somewhat similar to the town where they'd encountered the deadly bubonic plague just a few time jumps ago.

"No! Please! Not the plague again!" Ray cried out. He pawed at the temporal transporter around his neck and spun the dials, but without the time machine, it was no use.

A group of people rounded the corner of the square. To Ray's surprise, they looked completely healthy. Fancy, even. The women were dressed in fine Renaissance clothing—fit with long dresses, pearls, and ornate braids. They stared at him with a certain air of disgust. Ray covered his bare chest in embarrassment. At the other end of the square, a welcoming castle shimmered in the sun.

A castle? Hmm . . . Maybe if I plead my case to a king, he could help me.

He passed a sign hanging above one of the storefronts. It read "Magazzino Generale di Milano."

"Milan, huh? Must be in Italy," Ray said to Meekee.

He walked down the small road leading to the castle entrance. He passed under the wrought iron main gate and followed around the perimeter until he ended up outside a hidden side entrance.

Above the iron door, a miniature water wheel carried water from the castle roof down into the locking mechanism. The whole thing was ingeniously rigged to spin the handle with nothing but gravity.

Whoa. Cool!

Ray knocked on the wood of the door, but no answer.

"Mr. Becker?" Ray said. "Are you in here?"

There was no response.

Figured it was a long shot.

He creaked the gate open and couldn't believe his eyes. Inside was an incredible workshop. Wooden devices, inventions, and rows upon rows of gorgeous paintings sat on every table, pedestal, and easel in the room.

"Meekee!" the little alien whispered.

"I was just about to say the same thing, buddy," Ray said in total awe.

Parked in a seat next to one of the canvases, an older man

slumbered. He wore a velvet cap pulled down over his eyes. A long gray beard poked out and stretched down the man's chest. The beard, on top of the paintings and makeshift mechanical devices, was the last piece of the puzzle for Ray.

"DA VINCI?!" Ray shouted.

"AHHH!" The man shot up from his slouch with a start. The velvet cap flew off his head as he clutched at his heart.

Without the hat, Ray was sure. It was him. Ray had kept a poster of him up in his room for years. He knew that he should steer clear of talking to da Vinci in case he were to mess with any of his genius creations by accident, but he couldn't contain himself.

"HOLY MOLY! It *is* you!" Ray jumped up and down with delight. "I told them! I've always wanted to meet you!"

"Mamma mia! Cosa ci fai qui, ragazzo? E dov'è la tua maglietta?" da Vinci inquired.

"Oh, Mr. da Vinci! Words cannot express how happy I am to see you right now!" Ray said. "Leo? May I call you Leo?"

Ray wrapped the old man in a hug. Da Vinci pushed him off with a surprisingly sturdy shove.

"No, no! You don't understand!" Ray said. "I'm your biggest fan! I once got in so much trouble after I tried to re-create your Last Supper painting on the wall in my dining room. My dad grounded me for weeks! And you're not going to believe this, but I traveled here in a time machine! It's not here right now. And I'm not really sure how I got separated from my friends.

But if anybody can help me get back, it's gotta be you!"

Da Vinci blinked his eyes, clearly dumbfounded by the shirtless child who had just invaded his private studio.

Ray kept going. "You know, everybody always gives credit to that Thomas Edison guy, but I always said da Vinci. Da Vinci was ahead of his time!"

"Non capisco una parola di quello che stai dicendo in questo momento," da Vinci replied.

"Oh um. I'm sorry. Mi italiano is-a no good-a," Ray said.

Meekee popped up from Ray's pocket and climbed onto his shoulder. He hung his front two legs out and chirped with delight.

"Da Vinkee! Da Vinkee!" the little alien said.

"No, Meekee," Ray corrected. "His name is da Vin-chi! Chi!"

The second Meekee came into view, da Vinci's eyes had illuminated with wonder. The inventor blew right past Ray, grabbed Meekee off his shoulder, and raced to other side of the room.

"Hey! Wait a second! Give him back! He's mine!" Ray protested. But da Vinci completely ignored him.

"Never meet your heroes, I guess," Ray muttered to himself.

Da Vinci carried Meekee across the room to another painting station he had set up in the corner. A bowl of fruit sat perched up on a small marble pedestal. With one swift karate chop, da Vinci knocked the bowl off and sent the apples and pears rolling across the glistening floor.

He set Meekee down gently in the center of the pedestal and flung open a pair of curtains, letting the warm Italian light pour in through the window, right onto the little alien. Meekee purred with delight.

Da Vinci pulled out a paintbrush, a palette, and some colored oil pigments. Within seconds, he whipped together the perfect shade of green. He settled into position, held up a thumb, squinted an eye at Meekee, and then set his paintbrush down on the canvas.

Of course Meekee gets all the attention. If I were tiny and cute and an alien, maybe people would pay attention to me, too.

"Um, Mr. da Vinci, sir?" Ray said. "I know you might not be able to understand me, but there's gotta be a way you can help me out. I'm supposed to be helping my friend find her dad but—"

"Il tuo piccolo animaletto qui. Che esemplare unico. Sarà un ottimo soggetto!" da Vinci interrupted.

Ugh. What's the point of meeting a living genius if I can't even understand what he's saying?

Ray felt a sharp buzz in his pocket.

Oh yeah! The iPhone 42! Forgot I had this thing.

He dug his hand in and pulled out the smooth, rectangular device.

"Italian language detected," the phone's automated voice system said. "Would you like to translate?"

"Um . . . Yes? Please?" Ray replied.

"Please align the device with language source," the phone instructed.

"Uh, okay?" Ray aimed the body of the phone toward the back of Leonardo's head. He was too distracted with bringing the brushstroke Meekee to life to notice.

"Girati un po' a sinistra, *please. The light is much better this way*," da Vinci said, nudging Meekee on the pedestal a few degrees to the left.

Whoa. It automatically translates?! That's so dang cool!

Ray cleared his throat and spoke loudly into the back of the phone.

"Mr. da Vinci, sir? Can you understand me?" Ray asked.

Da Vinci's painting hand froze against the canvas. He turned to Ray with a stunned expression.

"You've suddenly learned Italian, I gather?" he said, the English seeming to come directly from his mouth, despite his lips still sounding out Italian words.

Ray quickly stashed the phone in his front pocket. "Uh . . . yes! I just learned Italian from hearing you! Pretty impressive, huh?"

". . . You learned Italian just in the last few minutes?" da Vinci said with an incredulous expression.

"Why do you say it like that?" Ray asked. "Do I not look like a brilliant genius to you?"

Da Vinci looked him up and down. *"Well, for one thing, you're covered in cow poo."*

"Meekee Meekee Meekee!" the baby alien said from on top of the pedestal.

Without thinking, Ray turned in Meekee's direction, causing the phone to also face the little alien.

"Meekee Meekee Mee—*Raymond. We really mustn't interfere with the timeline.*"

Ray's eyes grew wide. The voice coming out of the phone sounded deep and intelligent.

". . . Meekee?" Ray said. "Is that your real voice?"

"*Yes, my dear Ray,*" the little alien replied. "*Now, remember what your doppelgänger from the future instructed. It's imperative that we don't leave any impressions on the past.*"

"You're so . . . articulate." Ray was caught completely off guard. "I thought you were a baby, Meekee!" He stumbled backward, knocking a tray filled with black paint pigments all over his backside.

"*Careful, there! That's good paint!*" da Vinci scolded.

Ray tripped on the floor, falling backward and landing with a thud directly onto a perfectly Ray-size canvas that had been positioned on the floor.

"*What in the world are you doing?!*" da Vinci shouted. "*You've ruined an entire canvas of fine sheepskin!*"

"I'm so sorry!" Ray said. He lay completely splayed out on the floor and felt an ache in his rear end. He tried to stand up but ended up slipping again and landing even further splayed out in a snow angel pose.

"*Hold on a second . . . ,*" da Vinci said. He left Meekee on the pedestal and took a few curious steps toward Ray's canvas. "*Don't move a muscle, dear boy.*"

Da Vinci stepped back and examined the full body print Ray had left in black paint on the otherwise empty canvas.

"*I think you might be onto something here,*" da Vinci admitted. He pulled out a sketch pad and drew wildly, drawing Ray's proportions in the two positions.

Uh, did I just become the inspiration for one of da Vinci's most famous drawings?

CHAPTER
SEVENTEEN

Viv woke up on the floor of the time machine feeling like she'd just ridden every roller coaster at the Groom Lake County Fair—and the rickety ones twice. Parts of her hair had ended up stuck to her mouth. She managed to prop herself up onto her dizzy knees and quickly realized that she didn't have to jostle for space like she normally did whenever the time portal made a sudden landing somewhere. Her friends were missing in action.

No. This can't be happening. I lost them?!

The navigation screen of the time machine flashed bright red. Complicated error messages displaying endless strands of data scrolled by as Viv felt a pit of despair building up in her gut. She zeroed in on Elijah's coordinates and pulled at the lever, but the machine wouldn't respond.

No, no, no! Come on! Please don't be broken!

She slammed her hands down on the dashboard.

"I told them to stop fighting over the controls!" she said

out loud to no one. Her voice echoed off the empty time machine.

This is all my fault! I let them come with me on this hare-brained mission to find my dad!

Now they're out there, stranded! I don't even care about finding him anymore! I just want my friends back!

She instantly felt the heat building up behind her eyes as her powers threatened to break through.

No, I need to stay in control of myself.

Realizing that freaking out wouldn't do anything to help the current situation, she took a deep breath and settled back in front of the navigation screen.

The current location of the time machine put her at December 17, 1905. The GPS indicator read latitude 46° 56′ 52.44″ N, and longitude 7° 26′ 59.64″ E.

Guess I'm somewhere in the Northern Hemisphere.

1905? Pre World War I. The Great Influenza hasn't hit yet. I should be okay, right?

Viv spun around on her heels and pulled down on the lever. The dented doors to the time machine creaked open into a private study filled with wall-to-wall chalkboards.

Waiting just outside the time machine doors, a man stared back at her with a stupefied expression, his knees shaking with fear. His mouth hung open, and the piece of chalk from his hand clattered to the floor.

His hair was missing its iconic white hue, but even in this

dark brown shade, the scruffy, unruly shape of his 'do was unmistakable.

". . . Einstein?" Viv said.

His knees wobbled as he gulped before answering.

"Ja?"

Viv's jaw fell open, and her expression lit up with momentary shock. She was completely and utterly starstruck. It wasn't long before her knees were shaking, too.

"Oh my goodness," Viv said. She did her best to remember the elementary German she had learned from a Languages around the World workshop she and Charlotte had taken together back in the fifth grade. "Um, um . . . Mein name ist Viv."

"Viv?" Einstein repeated.

Hearing her own name come out of the genius's mouth felt completely surreal. She nodded in astonishment.

"Call me Albert. Meine Englische . . . ," he said. "It is nicht perfekt."

"Oh, das okay," Viv said. "Meine Deutsch is also nicht so gut."

"Und who are you?" Einstein asked in his heavy accent.

"Well, um—" Viv began to say.

She considered it for a moment.

Hmm . . . I can't disrupt the timeline, but I could really use his help in figuring out how to get this machine back up and running. I have to be smart about this . . .

"I'm a figment of your imagination, Mr. Einstein," Viv said.

"Mein . . . imagination?" Einstein said, a knot sprouting between his eyebrows.

"Ja, Mr. Einstein. A vivid hallucination. That's why my name is Viv."

"Ah . . . Mein mind ist playing tricks . . . I suppose I have been vorking hard lately . . . Und . . . vat is diese Maschine?" Einstein said, pointing at the open doors of the time machine.

"It's a, um . . . a prototype! A machine that your subconscious created!" Viv said. "It's a time machine!"

"Ein *time machine*?" Einstein repeated. "I alvays zought it vas impozible!"

"Yes, it is impossible," Viv said. "But in your dreams, it's real!"

Einstein stoically examined the time machine.

Did he even understand me?

With a sharp tug, Einstein yanked off a piece of the dented paneling on the side of the time machine, exposing a bevy of wires and circuit breakers.

Whoa! Hey, now!

Viv considered stopping him, but it was Albert Einstein, for crying out loud.

If I were going to trust anyone with an advanced piece of revolutionary scientific discovery, it would be him.

He examined the inner mechanisms of the machine and turned to Viv with a skeptical expression.

"Diese machine, it vorks?" Einstein said.

"Well, usually. But I seem to have broken it," Viv said. "But enough about me . . . What are you working on?"

"Äh, hmm," Einstein pondered. "Äh . . . es ist . . . how you say, theory? Theory of mine."

The walls surrounding him were covered in vast chalkboards, each more blanketed in mathematical scribblings than the last. Einstein motioned to the complex scrawling and tapped his foot impatiently.

"Äh . . . I hypothesize that und relationship exists . . . how you say, zwischen Materie und Energie gibt . . . at zee atomic level," Einstein said, fiddling with the ends of his mustache in deep thought. "But I cannot quite . . . nail it down."

Oh my gosh. I think I know what he's talking about.

Viv looked over the board. The equations at the top of the proof were complicated, but Einstein had managed to simplify the concept to an extent where Viv recognized the theorem.

No way! Even I know this one. Everyone knows this one!

Back when she was a student at Groom Lake Middle, before the chaos of Area 51 had sunk its teeth into her life, Viv had gotten special permission from her physics teacher, Mr. Patterson, to prove Einstein's theory of relativity as a class presentation. She knew the sequence of equations like the back of her hand.

Should I help him solve it? Will that alter the timeline? I mean . . . he's meant to solve it anyway, right? What does it matter if he gets a little help? Technically, he's still the one who solved it!

"If you'll allow me," Viv said, taking a step toward the board. "I think your subconscious might know what you're missing." She extended her hand to receive a piece of chalk.

"Oh?"

Einstein looked over all of his handiwork on the chalkboard up until that point. He puckered his lips. He looked back at the time machine and then to the little girl who arrived in it. Reluctantly, he passed Viv a stick of chalk. She treated it like a sword in her hand. With a single deep breath, she went to work. She simplified. Then simplified again. Until all that was left was one compact equation. Viv underlined it with a few swipes of chalk, dusted off her hands, and put her fists on her hips.

"There you have it," she said triumphantly. "E equals MC squared!"

Einstein, mouth agape, approached the blackboard in complete and total awe.

". . . Could diese really be zat simple?" he said. Viv watched as his eyes flitted over every single variable, making sure that the math checked out. After a few moments, he snatched up Viv's hand and shook it exuberantly.

"Wunderkind! You've changed zee world of physics! Ausgezeichnet!" Einstein said.

"It's not me, Mr. Einstein," Viv said. "It's all you. I'm just a hallucination from your brain, remember?"

Einstein stroked at his mustache.

"I did do quite ein bit of vork on diese . . . ," he said proudly. "Can I . . . how you say . . . repay you . . . er . . . I mean me?"

"Well . . . ," Viv said. "There is one thing. I could use your help getting this machine working again."

Einstein gestured to the time machine and raised one of his bushy eyebrows.

"May I?" he asked.

"Of course!" Viv said.

Einstein rummaged through the core of the machine, examining and reorganizing parts. Viv watched in amazement as he practically taught himself electrical engineering before her very eyes. He meticulously rerouted various wires and tested every circuit along the way. Eventually, after a few dozen alterations, the screen on the dashboard chirped to life, displaying the functional screen settings from before.

"Yes!" Viv said. "You did it!"

"Of courze I did! It is mein ovn imaginazion after all," he said with a smile.

"Wait . . . Mr. Einstein," Viv said. "Could you help me with one more thing?"

He nodded. Viv offered a hand and led him inside the time machine. She pulled up the data on her mom's list of time jumps and coordinates. One massive number about six digits longer than the rest was listed as Cassandra's current location.

"This huge number . . . ," Viv said. "I think it's been scrambled up. Would you be able to calculate someone's position from this?"

He looked at the tracking data, showing all of the previous coordinates in the travel log. Viv twirled a lock of her hair nervously around her finger, peeking over his shoulder. She watched as the world's greatest scientific genius ran calculation after calculation, trying out different coefficients and scribbling wildly into the tiny pocket-size journal. Eventually, he tore out a sheet and folded it up.

"Here you are," he said. He handed over a piece of paper with a timestamp and its corresponding GPS coordinates.

Viv looked over his findings. Her eyes widened at what he'd written down—the exact same number that Viv already had.

"You're telling me this super-long number *is* a time coordinate?" Viv asked.

"Ja!" Einstein said. "Like I alvays zay, make efferyzing as zimple as pozible, but not zimpler."

Of course! It's just a big fat date! So Mom must be REALLY far into the future!

"Truly, Mr. Einstein," Viv said. "I really can't thank you enough."

"It is I who schould be zhanking you!" he said, slapping a happy hand against the chalkboard.

Viv waved goodbye, pulled the lever for the doors closed,

and set her temporal transporter to the first coordinate in the log.

Now to get to my friends, find Mom, and get back home.

Hope they all haven't been turned into sand . . .

When the doors opened, Viv saw nothing but sand.

"No!" she said. "Elijah? Elijah?! Is anybody here?!"

Her voice drowned out in the lapping wind and the cold.

Was Einstein wrong? No. He couldn't be!

Just as her heart began to sink, she spotted a set of footprints trailing down the dune.

Could it be?

She hustled over the ridge. Her eyes fell upon a strange sight: a vintage-looking airplane flanked on both sides by two men. Down below by the flyer's wheels, a smaller figure looked to be tinkering with some tools.

It could only be one boy.

"Elijah!" she shouted.

He turned his head in her direction. Even from this far away, she could see his gleaming white smile below a pair of old-timey pilot's goggles.

"Viv!" he called back.

The two took off sprinting toward each other across the sand. When they finally made impact, Elijah threw his arms around her. The hug was so tight, Viv was sure he'd be able to notice just how loudly her heart was pounding. Elijah grabbed her hand and led her back down the dune, toward the sand-dusted aircraft and the two men standing on either side of the wings.

"Hey! I want you guys to meet someone!" Elijah said.

He draped an arm around each of the men.

"Viv, allow me to introduce Orville and Wilbur," he said. "Orville and Wilbur, this is my friend Viv."

"Orville and Wilbur?" Viv said. "You mean . . . *the* Orville and Wilbur?"

"That's right!" he said with a smile.

"Another kid?" Wilbur said. "Where on earth do you keep coming from?!"

"I'm sorry to cut this short, but, Elijah, we gotta go!" Viv said.

"Why?" he said.

"I have the . . . uh . . . machine, so we can go find Charlotte and Ray!" Viv said.

"Say no more!" Elijah said. He grabbed her hand and pulled her back up the dune. "Sorry, fellas! But we gotta run!"

"Hey! What about my jacket?" Orville objected.

"I'll keep it safe for you!" Elijah said over his shoulder.

"Elijah!" Viv whispered as they ran. "Did you just steal a jacket from one of the Wright brothers?"

"It's a gift for my dad. And trust me, after today, those

two brothers will have enough money to buy a thousand jackets."

The two hopped into the time machine as Viv took over the controls, typing coordinates into the system.

"Where to next?" Elijah said.

"First we're picking up Char and Ray," Viv said. "Then we're meeting up with my mom and getting the heck home."

"But, Viv? What about your dad?" Elijah said.

She took a deep breath, facing for the first time the likely reality that they would never find him.

I can't risk anyone else's life on this plan anymore. I want to find him . . . more than anything. But I'm being selfish. Chasing after what I want isn't worth putting my friends in danger.

"Right now, I'm only worried about getting everybody back home safe." She pulled the lever to the door closed behind them.

"Can you believe that I got to meet the Wright brothers?" Elijah said. "I think I helped them with their first flight!"

"You're not gonna believe who I just met," Viv said with a grin.

✳ ✳ ✳ ✳ ✳

The second Viv and Elijah landed, the entire time machine vibrated. An impossibly loud sound coming from the basement shook the pieces that had been weakened from the cannonballs and sand blasts. Elijah cupped his hands around his ears. Viv shrugged and stepped out of the doors.

"Charlotte, we're here!" Viv called out.

The two stepped down the same staircase and hallway that led to the lower level, following the raucous piano sound. When they reached the bottom, Charlotte, who had her head buried in her hands, noticed them immediately.

"Finally!" Charlotte cried. "Took you guys long enough. One more round of banging on the keys, and I was about to smash that piano!"

"Charlotte?" Viv pointed to the man hunched over the grand piano. "Who is that?"

"It's Beethoven," Charlotte replied.

"Whoa, really?" Elijah said.

"Did you talk with him?" Viv asked.

"Yeah, but he can barely hear anything," Charlotte said.

"What?" Viv shouted over the music.

"I said, he can barely hear anything!" Charlotte shouted back.

"What'd you say?" Elijah said even louder.

Charlotte let out a huff, hooked her arms through Viv's and Elijah's elbows, and made for the time machine.

"Let's get outta here," she said.

"Ray, where the heck is your shirt?" Viv asked.

Back in Renaissance-era Italy, Ray was covered in paint.

"At least I still have my pants on!" Ray said. He pointed to a man who was furiously sketching away on a nearby table, too focused to even notice the time machine full of kids that had just arrived in his workshop. "And look at the sketch he did of me!"

"And who is he?" Viv asked.

"What? Don't you recognize him?" Ray said. "Guys, that's Leonardo da Vinci! Look!"

Propped up on one of the wooden easels was a first draft of da Vinci's legendary sketch, *The Vitruvian Man*.

"Ray . . . are you telling me that, somehow, YOU were the inspiration for *The Vitruvian Man*?" Viv asked.

"I guess so!" he replied.

"But it doesn't even really look like you?" Elijah said, scratching a fingernail against the charcoal drawing.

"Okay, so maybe da Vinci took a few creative liberties with the sketch," Ray admitted.

"A few?" Elijah said. "You mean, like, the long hair?"

"And the muscles?" Viv added.

"And the movie-star good looks?" Charlotte said.

"OKAY! OKAY! I get it!"

"Come on, Ray," Viv said. "We don't have any time to waste. Einstein triangulated my mom's coordinates! So, get your butt in that time machine, and let's get moving!"

"But what about da Vinci?" Ray asked.

"What about him?" Viv said.

"We need to bring him with us!"

"What? Are you kidding?" Elijah asked.

"Imagine all the amazing inventions he could create in the modern era!" Ray proposed.

"I don't think they even have toilets here yet," Charlotte said. "Must be some kind of inventor to still be pooping in a hole."

"That man's a genius. He doesn't need to concern himself with where people go to the bathroom!" Ray argued.

"Enough!" Viv said. "I manage to track you down through all of known history, and you guys are talking about toilets? We're all finally together. It's time to go!"

"But—but—" Ray stammered.

"No buts! Now, grab Meekee and let's get out of here!" Viv said.

Even the tiny alien seemed to be enjoying himself on their fun little side trip. He was nibbling on sun-ripened grapes atop a beautiful marble pedestal. Ray gave Meekee a squeeze, sending the grapes stuffed in his cheeks flying across the room.

"Meekee!" the green ball of fluff protested.

"I know, buddy, I'm sorry," Ray said. "I don't wanna go, either."

"Aw, Meekee sounds so sad," Elijah said.

"Trust me, you don't wanna hear his real voice," Ray replied.

"Real voice?" Elijah asked. "What do you mean?"

"I'll explain later," Ray said.

Viv hustled everyone back into the time machine, pulled out her Einstein note, and typed in the next set of digits.

One more stop.

I hope Mom's still alive.

CHAPTER EIGHTEEN

The second the metal doors opened, the heat from outside rushed in and threatened to turn the four kids into instant raisins. And unfortunately, the view wasn't much better than the temperature. For what seemed like miles, a nightmarish scape of destruction stretched out before them. To their left, an avalanche of rocks cascaded down the side of a cracked-open volcano. On the right, huge fissures of shattered earth split open in front of them, creating a latticelike web of crevices leading down to who knew where. The air smelled like death, and small fires broke out among the countless piles of ash.

The four kids crowded around the doors, staring out onto the apocalyptic wasteland that welcomed them with terrifying arms. A sinking feeling nearly brought Viv down to her knees.

Oh no. This *is where Mom is?*

"Are you sure Einstein knew what he was talking about?" Charlotte said.

"He got me back to you guys, didn't he?" Viv said. "Why would he be wrong about this?"

"Yeah, but there's no way your mom would try and stick around here," Charlotte replied. "This place doesn't look . . . super survivable."

"Hey, guys? What's up with the sun?" Elijah asked. He pointed toward the sky.

Instead of the normal yellow light shining against a blue backdrop, a gigantic red ball of flames seemed to be tickling the planet's atmosphere. There was no doubt in Viv's mind that something very, very bizarre was happening, and they were unfortunate enough to be witnesses.

"Are we sure we're still on Earth?" Ray questioned.

"We must be, right? I don't think the time machine can do space travel," Viv said.

She took a few steps back inside and leaned over the time machine dashboard, scrolling through the data log to see where their chronological coordinates ended up. At first, she scrolled. And then she scrolled some more. The sheer number of zeroes showing their timestamp made her jaw drop.

"Guys . . . ," Viv said. "I think we might be billions of years in the future."

"*Billions?*" Ray repeated. "No way."

"But why is the sun so red and giant?" Charlotte said.

"Because now it's a red giant!" Viv said.

"Right. That's what I said."

"Don't you guys know what happens at the end of a star's life cycle?" Viv asked. "It'll keep growing and growing as it runs out of fuel until eventually, the whole thing collapses onto itself and plunges the Earth into an uninhabitable chunk of rock!"

"If you think your mom might be here, Viv, we should probably go find her and get out of here as quickly as we can," Elijah said.

A dozen more boulders came crashing down into the Earth's crust around them. The fires were encroaching even closer to where the time machine was parked. Even spending just a few minutes there could spell certain doom.

"You guys stay here," Viv instructed. "I'll go search for Mom. It's way too dangerous for the rest of you."

"We're coming with you," Elijah said firmly, leaving no room for debate.

"No chance," Viv said. "I'll take Meekee but that's it. The rest of you stay here."

"Meekee? Why just Meekee?" Ray asked.

"Well, if any of the rest of you have Roswellian powers, now would be the time to let me know," Viv said.

Her friends all sighed.

"Sounds fair to me," Charlotte said. "I'm not going out there."

Ray peeled Meekee off his shoulder and handed him to Viv. He cuddled up against her cheek.

"Come on, buddy," Viv said, "We'll be back in ten minutes. If it takes any longer, I want you guys to get out of here."

Another boulder suddenly smashed down next to the time machine, nearly crushing Viv's hand as she held the doorframe.

"On second thought, let's make it five minutes," Viv said.

Just as she headed for the door, she felt someone catch her hand. It was Elijah.

"Viv . . . ," he said. "Be careful out there."

The concern in his voice was palpable. In fact, it made Viv feel even more afraid than she already did. She didn't want him to let go of her hand.

"I will," she replied, unsure if she could truly promise that.

The doors shut, enclosing her friends in the only upright structure that promised any amount of safety. She and Meekee were alone. She locked eyes with him.

"Okay, Meekee," Viv said. "I'm still learning how to use my gaenfouaureoqnagesrpt, so I'll need your help."

I hope I said that right.

Meekee nodded excitedly.

"All right, here's the plan," Viv said. "I want you to get on top here and create a force field over the time machine to keep you and the others safe. Keep it going no matter what. Can you do that for me?"

"Meekee! Meekee!" the little alien squealed with delight.

"And you be careful, too! Ray would never forgive me if something happened to you," Viv said.

"Meekee!"

"I hope that's a yes," Viv said.

She set him atop the roof and watched. With a little wiggle of his butt and a concentrated groan, the green light first enveloped his body and then extended out over the top of the time machine.

"That's good, Meekee! Keep that up!" Viv instructed. "I'll be back soon!"

She focused her mind as she took her first few steps out into the desolation.

I just gotta find Mom. And then we'll get out of here.

She took a deep breath, just like she had seen the older Vivian do before completing her telekinetic puzzle. With a squeeze of her fists, Viv could feel the energy flowing through her body. It felt like a wave of bubbles rising up through her bloodstream.

She centered herself and collected the ripples of power into her mind. She could feel the little bursts of energy combining with the emotional rush in her brain.

Focus, Viv. Just like Megdar said. Feel the desire in your soul. Now combine it with your feelings.

Like a tiny extraterrestrial umbrella, the meager green force field was barely big enough to cover the top of her head. It wasn't long before the first rock pinged off the floating green plate, saving her from what definitely would've been a nasty bruise.

Wow! It's working! I actually feel like I'm in control!

Viv took a few more steps forward before a massive chunk of iron came tumbling down, putting a decent-size dent into the green umbrella.

Okay. Well, that's humbling.

She wandered through the wasteland, dodging the majority of the hazards while trying not to sweat to death. The sun glared down on her and made her skin glow with an eerie coat of red. But she kept trudging. Eventually, she managed to reach a fork in the crust's cracks. Below the surface, a bubbling river of lava churned with a dangerous glow. She looked back over her shoulder and squinted. She could barely make out the tiniest green light—Meekee still dutifully doing his job. But then, something on the periphery of her vision caught her attention.

Just a few feet away, stranded on a flat piece of stone between the current of magma, a human figure sat hunched over.

"Mom!" Viv cried out, taking a few running steps toward the figure.

It was her. Bruised and looking exhausted. But it was her.

"Mom!" Viv shouted. "I'm here! It's me!"

Viv carefully leapt over the lava-filled trench and practically tackled her mom with a powerful hug.

Cassandra, her eyes closed, burst into tears.

"Viv . . . Oh my sweet Viv . . . ," she said, her voice cracking. "I was so close. I got so close to finding him. I really did try."

"I know, Mom," Viv said. "It's okay."

"I love you, Viv," her mother said. "I'm so sorry I left. I'm just glad I get to see you one last time before I die. Even if it is just a dream."

Viv pulled away and stared up at her mom, befuddled.

"No, Mom! This isn't a dream! It's me! I'm really here! In the flesh!"

Cassandra looked down with glazed-over eyes. She blinked a few times, breaking herself out of her exhaustion-induced stupor. Finally, recognition kicked in.

"VIV?!" she shouted. Her eyes changed from their dreamy state of delirium to a rigid clarity.

"Yes! It's really me!" Viv said.

"You went into the time machine?!" her mom shouted. "You are in so much trouble, young lady!"

Viv was speechless.

"And—and what's this?" Cassandra asked, pointing up toward the hovering, protective green disk floating over their heads.

Oh no.

In her haste to reach her mom, Viv forgot that she'd been using her powers at all. The guilt washed over her, and she felt the control of her gaenfouaureoqnagesrpt slip away The shield vanished into the air.

"I'm—I'm sorry," Viv muttered. "I forgot—I—"

"It's okay, it was an accident. Don't worry, sweetie," her mom said. "Guess it's just something I'll have to get used to."

Viv squirmed in her skin. She wanted to tell her mom everything. About her trip to Megdar's planet and all the new information she'd learned about her powers, but the idea of her mom realizing just how alien she was terrified her to her core.

"How on earth did you find me?" her mom asked, pulling her in for another tight hug.

"It's . . . it's a long story," Viv said. Tears were building up in her eyes.

"You should've stayed back," her mom said. "This is way too dangerous."

"You should've let me come with you from the start!" Viv argued.

"We'll talk about your punishment when we get home."

"Let's focus on the 'getting home' part first."

Her mom pulled away from the hug, her eyebrows knotting and her mouth twisting into a frown.

"We can't go back yet. What about your dad?" her mom asked.

"After everything it took to get to you, I don't think we'll be able to find him," Viv said.

Viv couldn't look her mom in the eyes. She didn't know

how to tell her that after all they'd been through, she was too scared to keep risking the lives of her friends on this crazy goose chase through time. They'd trusted her to get them back safely, and they'd already had too many close calls as it was. There was no promise that the next batch of coordinates would get them any closer to Ernest. Viv felt sick to think about losing the chance to know her dad so soon after she had even let herself hope about this possibility, but she didn't know what else to do.

So all she said to her mom was, "I'd rather have one parent than none."

"But—"

Before her mom could finish her sentence, a powerful gust of wind nearly blew them both off the rock and into the lava. Within a matter of milliseconds, a vortex of sand whipped around them, blocking out the light from the red sun.

"No! They're here!" her mom cried out. She wrapped Viv in her arms as the tornadoes funneled down into three points on the ground, just a few feet from where they were standing.

The three Nicks, still dressed in their white robes, materialized out of thin air. They circled Viv and her mother like a pack of vultures.

"Stay back!" Viv's mom instructed. But the threat only garnered a sinister snicker from the mysterious men. The three opened their mouths to speak, and only a single booming word echoed out.

"HALT."

With that single word, the lava flowing around them stopped in its tracks. And so did everything else. Every falling rock froze in place. The fracturing earth held still. Time itself seemed to stop in that moment.

"You've reached the end of the Earth's life cycle," the three of them said. They spoke in unison, creating a strange cacophony of perfectly synced-up voices all layered over one another. "You've come far enough."

"Who are you people?" Viv's mom asked.

The Nicks shared a shivering chuckle.

"Do you not recognize us? We are the seconds ticking by on your wristwatch. The grains of sand in an hourglass. The spirits of time itself. And we do what must be done."

"You do 'what must be done'?" Viv's mom said. "What does that even mean?"

"You humans are especially troublesome. There have been other timeline disruptors," the three said. "More of those who would wish to upset the carefully crafted balance we have been able to achieve. But it seems that mankind cannot help but be careless."

"We just want to get home, too," Viv said. "Please. Just let us leave, and we promise, you'll never see us again!"

"No!" her mom said. "We have one more place to go."

"Mom? What are you doing?" Viv cautioned.

"Please. Her father is still missing out there," her mom retorted. "His name is Ernest Becker and—"

"Oh, we know this *Ernest Becker*," the Nicks said, practically spitting out the name. "That man has caused more trouble than you could ever realize. We've been cleaning up after him for what feels like a millennium."

"Exactly," Viv's mom offered. "Let us collect him. We'll take him off your hands for you."

"It's too late now," the Nicks said. "He has been the cause of too much disturbance in the chronological domain. Ernest Becker will be destroyed. But we offer you a choice."

Viv gulped.

"Return to your present time," the three said. "Or face the consequences. The choice is yours."

Viv looked up at her mom, pleading with her eyes.

No. Please, Mom! Let's just get out of here!

Director Harlow planted her feet, puffed out her chest, and spoke slowly and clearly.

"We've come all this way. We're getting him back."

The three Nicks let out a collective grumbling sigh.

"So be it."

As swiftly as they arrived, the three robed men came together and joined hands. All at once, their bodies began to violently shudder, shaking the sandy particles that made up their very beings. The three figures fused together into a grotesque shape, a monstrous sand creature twenty times their normal size.

Still clinging to her mom, Viv stared up at the dune-size behemoth with a befuddled gape.

Oh crud.

CHAPTER NINETEEN

The sand monster was so gigantic, it nearly blocked out the sun. Somehow, the young boy, the man, and the elderly gentleman had merged into a colossus, formed by rippling waves of contorting sand to become a hulking, twenty-foot-tall titan.

"Stand back, Viv!" her mother instructed. From her waistband, Cassandra unclipped her dual plasma pistols and aimed them right at the creature's head. She held down the triggers, sending a barrage of particle bursts in the monster's direction. But each time one of the shots would make contact with the sand creature's body, it would blast straight through, only for the sand to re-form and fill in the gap a moment later. Cassandra tried again, this time aiming all the shots in one spot: right between the goliath's sandy eyes.

The hole was bigger this time, but still not big enough. A million more grains quickly flowed into the vacant spot.

CHRONOMETRIC ENTITIES NO. 001–003

Regenerative
abilities

Lethal touch

Ability to
merge
(theorized)

ALIAS: THE NICKS OF TIME

TRUE NAME: Unknown
ORIGINS: Unknown
CATEGORY: Highly dangerous

Very little is known about these ancient entities. Theorized to be
physical manifestations of time itself, Agents ▮▮▮▮ and ▮▮▮▮
believe they aim to permanently eliminate all anomalies to the time
stream. Discrete sightings in the years ▮▮▮, ▮▮▮, and the ▮▮▮
century have been reported but never confirmed.

If observed, DO NOT APPROACH.

DOWNLOADING...   REDACTED FILES   ALERT:
                                                CLEARANCE LEVEL 12 NEEDED

— THE CONTINUUM NAVIGATION WING —

One of only a few abandoned wings of the base. After Ernest Becker's unfortunate disappearance, former director Martinez deemed time travel to be too dangerous, and the Continuum Navigation Program was shut down. In order to power the time machines with enough energy to generate a time portal, this room requires the most electricity in all of Area 51.

ALERT:
CLEARANCE LEVEL 12 NEEDED

DOWNLOADING...   CONFIDENTIAL

TIME TRAVEL DEVICES

TIME MACHINE

Designed by head chronometrist Ernest Becker, these advanced machines use over one billion watts to generate powerful time portals, allowing the user(s) to move through time and space once a specific coordinate is typed into the dashboard.

TEMPORAL TRANSPORTER

A crucial gadget for successful time travel, these transporters allow for the safe passage and rearrangement of human atoms as they travel through time portals. When functioning properly, these devices share tracking data between a time machine and Area 51, no matter the wearer's position within the time stream.

RESEARCH & DEVELOPMENT
Gadget Log-2050

The Flight Suit
Gadget ID No. 0569643, version 18

Skipping the bulky wings and wasteful jet fuel from the original design, this device uses state-of-the-art reverse magnetic propulsion that allows the user to fly unencumbered at speeds of up to 2,500 miles an hour.

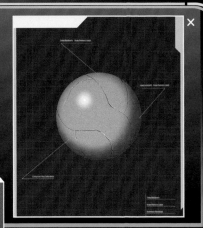

The Duplicator Amulet
Gadget ID No. 0612938, version 25

Instead of heavy bronze gauntlets, this wearable duplicator amulet links to the user's brain waves, allowing them complete control over an unlimited number of clones as well as the ability to link to the cognitive activity of others.

iPhone 42
ONLY AVAILABLE ON BASE

TRANSLATION MODE

An Area 51-exclusive update on the popular cell phone design, this handheld apparatus has over 1,000 functions. Cocreated by resident inventor Ray Mond and Chief of Robotics Joanna Kim, there isn't much this phone can't do.

CENTRAL BRAIN INTERFACE

"Mom, it's not working!" Viv cried. "It's no use!"

"It has to work!" she said, firing off another flurry of futile shots. "What other option do we have?"

The monster reared back its arms. Viv yanked at her mother's waist and pulled her out of the way just in time, as the sand beast slammed its fist down mere inches away from where they had been standing. The sand pounded into the ground and spouted up with a deadly spray of grains.

"Don't let any of the sand touch you!" Viv yelled. "They'll erase you from the timeline!"

"What? What do you mean?" her mom shouted back, rolling behind a sizable boulder for cover. "How do you know that?"

"Because I told me!" Viv said.

"What on earth are you talking about?"

"Older me told me! *I* told me!" Viv explained.

"Viv, that doesn't make any sense!"

Ugh. Forget it!

The two clambered up onto their feet, using the boulder as a temporary shield against the blasts of sand that the Nicks were aiming their way.

"Stay behind me, Viv," her mom said.

"Mom . . . I can protect myself, ya know!" Viv protested.

Cassandra readjusted the barrels of one of her plasma pistols.

"Those things aren't working!" Viv said.

"Well, what are we supposed to do? Not even put up a fight?" her mom said.

We're out of options.

I don't have a choice.

"Mom . . . I'm going to use my powers," Viv said.

Cassandra lowered her pistols for a moment, the color draining from her face.

"No way. Nuh-uh," she said.

"Why not?!"

"Because we don't even know anything about them yet!" Director Harlow objected. "What if they don't work?! What if you accidentally hurt yourself?"

"I know more about them than you think!" Viv said.

The boulder shielding them began to shake. Viv peeked out around the side of the rock. The abominable sand creature took a few steps forward, closing the distance, sending the ground quaking beneath every footfall. They were running out of time.

"Please. I can do this. I just need you to trust me," Viv said.

Her mom's eyes were unreadable. Cassandra sneaked a glance toward the lumbering monster headed their way. Viv could see the gears turning in her mom's head, calculating their odds of surviving this encounter with only the plasma pistols to protect them.

Viv couldn't help but think back to when her mom had asked Viv to trust her, too, before taking them to the time machine. She hadn't known how to answer her mom then with the betrayal and lies stacked so high between them. But now . . . now that she, too, couldn't bring herself to go after her dad for fear of her friends getting hurt . . . she thought she understood her mother a little better. All Viv could hope was that her mom would feel the same way about her.

Her mom let out an exhausted breath and slowly nodded.

"Do it," she said. "Go get 'em, Viv."

Viv took a deep breath in through her nose and let the air escape from her mouth. Everything Megdar told her ran through her head. She imagined she was back on the Roswellian planet, floating among all the bubbles and other extraterrestrial creatures. She concentrated her thoughts and imagined what it would be like if that beast got a hold of any of her friends. Or her own mom. She could feel the pain welling up inside of her, trickling in first through her eyes and then spilling down her nerve endings. Just like the pieces of a puzzle, Viv could feel her emotions, her soul's desires, and the radiant Roswellian energy all clicking together inside her mind. The powers burned inside of her, even hotter than the giant red sun beating down on her.

She strained, tightening all the muscles in her arms with every ounce of energy she could muster. The boulder shielding them lifted up slowly at first. But soon enough, Viv managed to get the entire massive rock hovering high above their heads.

It's working. I can do this!

She thrust her arms forward, telekinetically commanding the boulder to fly through the air like a bullet. Her mom watched in pure astonishment as Viv managed to cleave one of the sand monster's arms clean off. The sand was slower to grow back this time. Enraged, the Nick monster blasted another funnel of sand toward them. But Viv's reflexes kicked in. She pulled her arms into her sides, generating a protective bubble around her and her mom.

"Throw another!" her mom shouted.

Viv zeroed in on a particularly sharp hunk of rock that was sliding off a nearby cliff. Using only her mind, she peeled it off the mountainside and rocketed it toward the Nicks. This time, it sliced in right around the beast's sandy thigh, hacking a substantial hole in its left leg. The entire monster teetered, struggling to keep its balance on uneven footing. But Viv could already feel the fatigue creeping in.

"Viv! You're—you're unbelievable!" her mom said.

"Thanks, but I don't think I can keep this up much longer!" Viv said.

Her mom surveyed their surroundings. The general destruction was picking up speed, too. All the rocks that had been crumbling down the steep hillsides now slid with great speed. The lava from the volcanoes exploded up in geysers all around them, burning holes in the ground and making their safe zone of rock shrink with every passing moment.

"We need to retreat," she said. "There's no way the two of us can fight that thing off."

Just as the words left her mouth, the sand monster let out a terrible, earth-trembling growl. Its stomach undulated and rumbled with sickening vibrations. The titan opened its mouth and released a typhoon of projectile sand that crashed down on Viv's wavering force field. The strength of the surge was so powerful, Viv could feel her feet sliding backward on the uneven rocks. Her mom managed to catch her just in time, before her foot slipped off the edge and into one of the magma-filled crevices surrounding them.

"If we can just make it back to your time machine, maybe we can escape them!" her mom said.

"What about your time machine, Mom?" Viv said. "Didn't you come in on one? Is it nearby?"

"Mine is down for the count," she said, pointing toward a pile of rocks. Poking out from beneath the slabs, you could barely make out the glistening bits of metal. The entire thing had been crushed. Wires and metal stuck out from beneath the boulders like a bug squashed under a foot.

"That rockslide almost killed me," her mom said. "I managed to jump out at the very last second, but I've been stuck here since."

Viv looked back toward the direction she'd come from. An avalanche of stones had piled up on the path, blocking the way back.

"Wait a minute—you brought your FRIENDS here, too?!" her mom yelled.

"Yeah?" Viv said. "But how'd you know that? I told them to wait in the time machine."

"I don't think they listened to you!" Director Harlow said, pointing toward the sky behind the shadow of the sand monster.

Viv spun around on her heels and nearly had a heart attack. What looked like a million Charlotte clones had formed a tidal wave, all on a collision course with the Nick monster's back.

"VIV! WE'RE HERE!" the wave of Farlottes screamed in unison.

Each of the clones crashed into the side of the sand creature, instantly evaporating the second they made contact. Dozens after dozens of them disappeared into nothingness. Even just a brush against the sand erased them from existence. It wasn't long before there were none left. The real Charlotte, draped in her updated cloning amulet, watched in horror from the ground.

"Dang! That didn't go as planned!" Charlotte yelled.

"I thought I told you guys to wait in the time machine?!" Viv said.

"We got one look at that sand demon and figured you might need some help!" Charlotte replied.

Zooming around one of the geysers of lava, Elijah soared

through the air. It was the first time Viv had ever seen him fly without the full flight suit. Free from the bulky wings on his back, he whizzed through the air completely unencumbered, looking more like Superman than ever.

"How can we fight something we can't touch?!" Elijah shouted, narrowly dodging another swing of the behemoth's remaining arm.

"We need something else!" Charlotte shouted back, forming a new batch of clones beneath the monster's feet.

"Ray! What about the thing that Older Ray gave you back at Area 51?" Elijah asked from high above.

Ray, trailing a few yards behind, was completely out of breath, still shirtless, and running to catch up. He squealed with terror each time a rock landed even remotely close to him. He nearly tripped and fell into a pool of lava before he managed to take a spot hiding behind Viv's force field.

"You mean this thing?" Ray said in a huff, holding up the iPhone 42. "Older me never taught me how to use it! All I know is that it can translate foreign languages!"

"At least try *something*!" Viv implored, trying her best to keep the shield up.

"Like what?!" Ray said. "You want me to take its picture? Add it to my contacts?! Although, this would make a *great* TikTok."

Yeah, I don't think that's gonna help.

"We need to get out of here!" Viv's mom said.

"What about our time machine? Is it still standing?" Viv asked.

"I think so! Meekee's still holding up the force field!" Ray said.

"You guys left Meekee alone back there?!" Viv said.

"We didn't have a choice!" Ray protested.

The colossus turned its attention to Elijah. The boy flew in circles by its head, disorienting the beast as best he could. Blasts of dangerous sand pulsed through the sky. Elijah maneuvered like a fighter jet, twisting and weaving into the swaths of clear air.

Viv's mom stepped out in front of her daughter. "We need to hit it all at once!" she said. "Think you have one more in you, Viv?"

Viv nodded. She managed to spy another large rock next to Charlotte, who was busy amassing her next army of Farlottes. With a raise of her eyebrow, Viv flung the rock directly into the sand monster's head, leaving an enormous crater right where the creature's brain would be. The beast grumbled and grabbed at its head in pain.

Hoping to slow down the titan, Charlotte assembled an immense wall of clones. But they were no match for the stomping behemoth. Each plodding step the sand monster took, it crushed at least a hundred of the duplicates into dust. Director Harlow fired another volley of particle blasts, aiming for the weakened part of the creature's leg. The limb crumbled away, sending the chasing beast stumbling to the ground.

"Go now! While it's distracted!" her mom commanded.

Viv took the cue and let her force field drop off. All at once, Viv, her mom, and Ray took off sprinting back the way they came, scrambling over the rocks that had fallen in their path. Charlotte was close behind as Elijah followed suit in the air.

The sand monster roared in agony. Ripples began to spread all over its body. It trembled and shook with the force of a thousand earthquakes. Eventually, the buildup of sand exploded out of his mouth, sending a sand monsoon toward them.

The group of escaping humans rushed toward the tiny glowing green light of Meekee's force field off in the distance. Viv squinted and could just barely make out the alien straining and struggling to keep the shield up over the time machine.

"Wait for me!" Ray cried out. Viv turned back over her shoulder, watching as the tsunami of sand gained on them. Ray ran a few paces back, floundering in his attempts to jump over the cracks in the earth and still fumbling with the iPhone. Before the sand managed to get to him, Elijah swooped down and lifted him off the ground, zooming by to safety with the squirming Ray in his arms.

Thank goodness.

But with Ray safely in Elijah's hands, Viv had become the back of the pack.

She looked over her shoulder. The crest of the wave was

only a few yards behind and gaining distance fast. Her eyes zeroed in on the curling tip that was inching toward her. She tried to pick up the pace, but her legs wouldn't go any faster. Viv watched in horror as a single grain of sand broke free from the rest. It surged through the air, aiming directly at the spot between her eyes.

If that thing touches me, I'll be gone forever.

No one will even remember me.

Viv closed her eyes, held her breath, and prepared to disappear from time completely.

CHAPTER TWENTY

WHOOSH!

A spout of flames rocketed past Viv's face and crystallized the single grain of sand into a microscopic shard of glass.

"WHOA!" she shouted. The heat nearly singed off Viv's eyebrows. Still sprinting, she tilted her head back, and her eyes widened as they followed the trail of fire up to its source.

Somehow, miraculously, Ray had managed to find the iPhone's flamethrower feature just in time.

"Whoops!" Ray cried. Dangling from Elijah's arms as he flew through the air, Ray barely had control over the jet of fire. It shot out of the phone and doused the wave of sand in an orangey blaze, instantly transforming the crest into a crystalline glass wall.

"YES!" Charlotte shouted. "Way to go, Ray!"

"Best cell phone feature *ever!*" Ray exclaimed. "But I don't know how to turn it off!"

"Don't turn it off! Keep that thing going!" Viv called. She, Charlotte, and her mom still raced down on the ground below, leaping over the ever-growing chasms beneath their feet.

Ray adjusted the phone in his hand, sending the stream of fire sweeping up into the air and catching the end of Elijah's shoelaces on fire.

"HEY! Watch it!" Elijah shouted, rubbing his heels together to snuff out the embers.

"Sorry!" Ray cried. "Can you get me any closer?!"

Elijah took the cue and turned his shoulders. Even with Ray weighing him down, he still moved through the air with ease. The two boys flew over the top of the rushing sand, spewing enough of the inferno to stop it in its tracks. The tidal wave came to a standstill, looking more like a glistening art installation than a typhoon of deadly time sand.

Next was the colossus itself. This time, Ray turned the phone sideways, aiming the full power of the fiery blast at the sand monster's feet. As the burst of fire coated its toes, the conjoined Nicks howled. The flames crept up the monster's intact leg and spread toward its torso. The beast wailed in agony as the grains of sand that made up its body fused together in the heat. Eventually, the rising fire made it up to the monster's neck and spread across its face, freezing the behemoth's mouth into a permanent glassy scream.

The insatiable fire curled up at the top of the beast's head, licking at the sky hungrily.

And with that, the entire Nick Monster had completely hardened into glass. With nothing left to consume, the flames faded away into the breeze.

It was quiet for a moment as everyone caught their breath.

"WOO-HOO!" Ray shouted. "Take THAT, sand monster!"

He and Elijah safely landed alongside Charlotte and Viv.

"Well done, boys!" Charlotte said, giving them each a rough slap on the back.

Viv hunched over, her hands on her knees, and gasped for air. She wiped a hefty layer of sweat from the top of her forehead.

Oh my gosh. We did it! We actually did it!

Before she could celebrate, the silence was broken by a loud *ZAP*. Director Harlow aimed her plasma pistol at the creature's chest and pulled the trigger. The burst shattered through the glass and sent fragmented shards pinging to the ground.

"Mom!" Viv said. "It's okay! We already beat it!"

"I'm not so sure about that," her mom replied. She motioned down by their feet. Already, the tiny shards of glass were bouncing and shaking, being pulled back together by some kind of invisible force. They piled up onto one another and rattled so violently that the individual grains started to break down and revert back to their sand state.

"I don't think it's dead," her mom said with an edge of concern. "We might've slowed it down a little, but eventually, that thing's gonna re-form."

"I don't want to be here when it does," Ray said.

"We shouldn't stick around any longer than we have to," her mom agreed.

"I'm with Director Harlow," Charlotte said. "Let's get the heck outta here!"

"Guys! Look!" Elijah said. He pointed up toward the sky.

The enlarged red sun looked even angrier than before. Miles-high flares writhed out of the surface like giant flaming worms.

"Forget the sand! The sun's gonna blow!"

"Great," Viv said. "Perfect timing!"

The group took off sprinting again. They rounded a few columns of stone, finally making it to the area where the kids' time machine initially landed.

"There it is!" Viv said.

Meekee, who was still guarding with his green force field, caught sight of the approaching group and jumped up and down with delight on the roof.

"Good boy, Meekee!" Ray said. "Good boy!"

"Meekee . . . Meekee . . ." The little alien sounded exhausted. Creating a force field big enough to protect the entire time machine from all the rocks and debris was clearly enough to zap all of his energy. Ray held out his hands and let Meekee fall into his arms, wrapping up the adorable alien in his embrace.

The kids and Director Harlow hustled into the open doors of the time machine.

The time machine doors closed on the five tightly packed travelers.

"We're headed home, right?" Ray said.

"No, not quite," Viv's mom said, scrolling through the dashboard. She furiously typed in a coordinate. "We have one more place to go."

"Do we have to?" Ray groaned.

"I think I know where Ernest is," Viv's mom said. "I was headed there before my time machine got destroyed."

"But, Viv, I thought you said it would be too hard to find him?" Elijah asked.

Viv looked between Elijah and her mom. She felt like her head was spinning.

"It's not impossible!" her mom protested.

"But we've been chasing after him all over history, too! And we haven't even come close!" Charlotte said. "We've seen evil monkeys, pirates, the plague, you name it. Who's to say this next stop will be right?"

"Listen. I was in the Bronze Age when I finally figured out that we forgot to accurately account for daylight saving time. I ran further calculations on his time loop and deduced the pattern. I know where he is now, but the second I solved it, my time machine got crushed! If you kids could just hold on for one more stop, I promise we'll go right home after that."

Squeezed into the time machine, Director Harlow had to reach across Ray to lay a hand on Viv's shoulder.

"Viv. Remember earlier? You said I needed to trust you about your powers, and I did," she said. "Now I need you to trust me."

There it was again. Her mom asking Viv to trust her. And she wanted to. But after being separated from her friends and attacked by a giant sand monster, the promise of finding her dad seemed like such a long shot.

"I—I don't want to put the rest of them in danger," she said, gesturing to her friends. "What if we quickly go back to the base, drop them off, and then go back out for Dad?"

"There's no time!" her mom rebuffed. "This is our last shot to save your dad. If he is at the next coordinate in the time loop, he probably won't stick around there for much longer."

"But couldn't he just stay there for a second?" Viv asked. "The Nicks of Time aren't even chasing after him anymore! They're made of glass right now!"

"Yes, but he doesn't know that!" her mom said. "Not to mention, who knows how long until the Nicks are able to re-form and come after him again? This is our only chance!"

Viv felt her heart being torn in two. Ray and Meekee gave her a flash of weary puppy-dog eyes.

"I—I don't know . . . ," Viv said.

BANG!

Something heavy impacted the side of the time machine, crumpling in part of the metal right next to the corner where Charlotte was huddled.

"WHOA!" Charlotte cried out.

Without Meekee's force field, the time machine was a sitting duck for all the destruction raging on outside.

"Viv? I need an answer!" her mom said. "That sun is gonna kill all of us if we don't decide on a place soon!"

Viv bit at the inside of her cheek. She looked up at Elijah and couldn't help but picturing his dad—Lieutenant Nicolás Padilla—a man who was one of the coolest and most talented pilots on planet Earth but still managed to make it to every single one of Elijah's baseball games. Her eyes passed over to Charlotte, who spent every weekend with her dad hiking, camping, and playing music around the campfires they built together. Then there was Ray, a boy whose dad had managed to fight off a horde of aliens with a homemade fart gun.

The aching in her own heart was too strong to ignore. All her life, she'd wanted to get to know her own father. And she knew her friends would want that for her, too.

Mom's right. We need to protect the people we care about. And I don't know if I could live with myself if we passed up on this chance.

It's now or never. We need to find him.

Viv let out a puff of air.

"Okay. Let's do it," she said. "We've come all this way."

Her mom stared deep into Viv's eyes. She wiped away a stray tear from her cheek and sprang back into action.

"You heard the woman!" Director Harlow said.

Ray, Charlotte, Elijah, and Viv nodded and adjusted their temporal transporters accordingly. With the final twist of Viv's dials, the electricity sparked to life inside of the trusty time machine that had managed to take them so far.

Just one more stop. One more chance to find Dad.

The currents of static flowed in through the ceiling, filling the interior compartment until finally, the time portal ripped open in a flash, allowing the five of them to escape the doomed Earth . . . just in the nick of time.

CHAPTER TWENTY-ONE

After the misery they'd just experienced, Viv half expected the doors of the time machine would somehow open up into a fiery pit filled with venomous snakes, razor blades, and scary clowns.

But instead, the doors opened to familiar sight.

They had landed on top of a stretch of sheet-vinyl flooring. The fluorescent lights in the ceiling cast a bluish-white glow. The distinct orange paint on the walls was still the same, and the air smelled sharp and unwelcoming, like a mix of various cleaning products and bleach.

Viv immediately recognized the place and reveled in the comfort of finally knowing where the heck she was.

A couple of years ago, during the first few weeks of sixth grade, Charlotte had somehow convinced Viv that it was a good idea for the two of them to try out for the volleyball team. But after one scrimmage, in her efforts to impress the coaches, Viv dove for a ball and accidentally dislocated her shoulder. The teachers watching in the gym rushed her to the hospital—Bald Mountain General. *This* hospital. It was the same hospital that she'd been going to all her life.

"Why are we in the hospital?" Viv whispered.

"Shhh," her mom said, placing a gentle finger to her lips. "We still need to stay out of sight."

Their time machine had landed tucked in a corner behind a light blue cubicle curtain. With the kids all crowded behind Viv trying to get a peek, Director Harlow was the first to take a step out. She walked with silent footsteps and slowly peeled back a corner of the curtain.

"Oh my . . . ," she said under her breath.

Viv was transfixed, watching her mom's back as she stood there staring out for what seemed like forever.

What does she see out there?

Is it a sick patient? Oh no. Is Dad in the hospital?

Or worse. Please don't tell me it's a scary clown.

After another half a minute, Viv could see her mom's shoulders start to rise and fall, almost as if she was crying.

"Mom?" Viv said.

Director Harlow let go of the curtain and spun back around to face the kids. She had, in fact, started to cry.

"Of course," her mom said, wiping a tear from her cheek.

"What is it?" Viv said. "What's out there?"

"It's the place he couldn't be . . . ," she said. "The moment he lost."

She pulled back the corner of the curtain again, this time, just wide enough so that Viv could peek into the hospital room.

Nothing seemed to be out of place. A young woman was lying on the hospital bed, clutching a small bundle of cloth close to her chest. Viv blinked a few times, adjusted her glasses on her nose, and squinted out for a better look at the part of the room she could see.

Is that . . . ?

No way.

It was her mom, or at least, another version of her mom, looking the same way she did in the old Polaroid she and her friends had found in the filing room. Her mom, the one lying on the bed, smiled down at the bundle of cloth in her arms. Viv could barely make out the tiny tuft of black curly hair poking out of the swaddled blanket.

"Is that . . . is that *me*?" Viv asked. Her mom nodded.

"And look," her mom said, adjusting the curtain another inch.

Hidden behind the heated bassinet and monitor screens, someone else was watching them—a man dressed in a three-piece suit. A gentle smile extended across his face.

Oh my god.

It was him. The same man she'd seen in the terrarium. The same man who spoke the words she'd been waiting to hear her entire life back in the Area 51 hallway.

It was Ernest Becker.

It was her dad.

Visiting her the day she had been born.

Viv's bottom lip started to tremble. She couldn't help it. The emotions rushed into her like a jolt of lightning. Her heart began to pound, and tears welled up in her eyes. She wanted to run out and tackle him, wrap herself up in his arms, and ask him a billion questions. But before she could, the squeal of the hospital-room door opening almost gave her a heart attack.

It was a nurse dressed in a set of orange scrubs. She entered with a clipboard. Director Harlow instinctually let go of the curtain, concealing Viv and the time machine full of kids once again.

"All right, Ms. Harlow," the nurse said to the woman lying in the hospital bed. "We're just gonna take you and sweet baby Vivian over to the next room to get her weighed and run a few tests. Feeling up for a little trip?"

"That sounds good to me," the young version of her mom said.

The nurse pushed on the bars behind the hospital bed. She maneuvered it out of the room and the door shut behind them with a gentle clack. It was quiet for a moment before Director Harlow pulled back the curtain.

". . . Ernest?" she said.

The man crouched behind the medical equipment stood up straighter. His eyes blinked in rapid succession.

"C-Cassandra?" His voice cracked at the sound of her name.

They took a few slow steps toward one another before the recognition kicked in. They collided into each other in an earth-shattering hug.

"Is this real?" he asked. "Is it really you?"

"It's me. I'm here," Viv's mom said. "I'm so sorry it took this long. I thought . . . I thought you were gone."

"*You're* sorry? *I'm* sorry!" Ernest said through tears. "I'm so sorry. Had I known you were pregnant, I never would've stepped foot into that time machine."

Viv had never seen her mom cry like this before. Cassandra sniffled and tried to choke back her tears.

"It's okay. I know," she said. "I'm not mad."

Ernest's eyes fell onto Viv. Instantly, she felt a shiver shake down her spine.

"Oh my goodness," he said. "Viv?"

Cassandra gave a sweet nod and ran her hand through the back of Viv's hair. "Go on, sweetie."

Viv ran into his arms and collapsed into his embrace. She sobbed on his shoulder, still feeling like she was in some kind of dream. Finally, after all the years she'd imagined him. Here he was. In the flesh.

After a long time, her dad pulled back from the hug, wiped away the happy tears collecting on his chin, and turned to Viv's mom with a furrowed brow.

"You took her along? You took our daughter into a time machine?!" Ernest asked.

"Of course not! You think I invited her?" Cassandra said with a laugh. "She sneaked into one of the machines after I left. She's a lot like you, ya know. Stubborn."

Ernest's eyes grew wide. "How much does she know?" he said. "About the compound?

Cassandra scoffed. "At this point, practically everything. You'd be surprised at how hard it is to keep a secret from her and her friends."

"Her friends?" Ernest asked.

"There's a lot we need to catch you up on," Cassandra said, motioning to the pack of onlookers still peeking out of the doors of the time machine. "Come on, kids. Don't be shy."

Charlotte, Ray, and Elijah slowly stepped out into the room, looking on at Ernest with pure shock and awe.

"Ernest—these are Viv's friends, Ray, Elijah, and Charlotte. They're Nicolás's, Desmond's, Al's, and Sabrina's kids."

"Are you kidding me? Al Mond and Sabrina had kids? So you two must be siblings, then!" Ernest said, pointing to Charlotte and Ray.

"EW!" Charlotte shrieked. "No way! I'm Sabrina and *Desmond's* kid!"

Ernest let out an uncontrollable belly laugh. "I'm just messing with you! Look at you all!" He threw his arms around the entire group of kids. "You're all so grown up!"

"It's nice to meet you, Mr. Becker!" Elijah said, his face squished up against Ray's in the bear hug. "We've been looking everywhere for you!"

"And boy, am I glad you found me!"

Cassandra took a few pensive steps around the hospital room in the spot where the bed had been just moments earlier.

"I remember this moment . . . ," she said. "It was right after I'd given birth to you, Viv."

She spun back to Ernest and laid her hands on his shoulders.

"I remember feeling your presence. But I always thought I was just imagining you . . . It must've been you! Why didn't you say something?!"

"Because I knew you would've come after me," he said. "I couldn't risk you getting lost, too."

"But what happened?" Director Harlow said. "Why didn't you ever come back?"

"I tried. I tried so hard. It was this," he said, reaching into his shirt. He pulled out the temporal transporter hanging around his neck. The device looked bizarre, completely different than the ones that Viv and her friends were wearing. Wires, additional knobs, and what looked to be a variety of gemstones were all jerry-rigged to the main body of the transporter. The whole thing was completely beaten up, worn down and abused from years—no—*millennia's* worth of use.

"My temporal transporter was damaged after my first

jump from the base. I landed in the year 1978, just like we had planned. Stuck around for a while, gathering information, enjoying a little music, but it didn't take me long to realize I was being followed. Tracked the entire time by these three people. They're the ones who destroyed the chronogeometer plate on my transporter that caused it to glitch and disconnect from my time machine. Strange beings. I call them . . . the Cloak Folks."

"The Cloak Folks?" Ray asked.

"Yeah," Ernest said. "It's a boy, a man, and an older guy. They're always dressed in these long, white robes and—"

"Oh, you must mean the Nicks of Time. That's what we've been calling them," Ray explained.

Ernest scratched at the back of his head. "Yeah, that's a lot better than Cloak Folks.

"Anyway, the three of them found me in 1978. They attacked me, and one reached out and touched my transporter. The chronogeometer plate instantly crumbled into sand. From that point on, the temporal transporter kept glitching, creating what seemed like randomized time portals and sending me to all these different places. I couldn't control any of it without the time machine. And with those guys chasing after me, I could never stay in one place for too long, anyway. They'd always find me."

"Holy cow!" Ray said. "They've been tracking you for over *twelve years*?"

"Yep. With every time jump, they'd always find me. Sometimes, it would be almost instantaneously. Other times, I would have at least a couple of minutes. One time, back in 603 BC, I had about ten minutes. That was a great day."

"Wait a second," Elijah said. "Are you saying that you've been time jumping every few minutes for the last *twelve* years?"

Ernest nodded.

"How are you not constantly puking?" Ray asked.

"Oh, I did at first," he said. "But you'd be surprised. After the first few years, I started getting used to it. So used to it, in fact, that I managed to get my sleep while traveling through the portals. It was the only way I could be sure they wouldn't find me while I was so vulnerable."

"But then how did you appear back at the base?" Viv said. "In the desert? And then again in the hallway?"

"Well . . . over the years of being stuck in the time loop, I finally managed to gather enough materials to retrofit this old broken temporal transporter. I equipped it with some of the elementary functions of the time machine. But that alone took nearly a decade. It wasn't until recently that I've been doing test runs, trying to return to the base in the present time."

"Is that why you were always flickering in and out?" Viv asked.

Ernest nodded and patted at the hodgepodge device hanging from his chest. "This thing certainly isn't perfect." He knelt down, coming face-to-face with Viv for the first time. She studied his features. A tiny mole above his left eyebrow made him look like he had a perpetually mischievous expression. His smile was soft and genuine, and his eyes were the same green color as hers. "Every single day, every single second, I've been trying to get back to you, Viv," he said. "You and your mom were always on my mind. In every millennium."

Viv collapsed into his arms for a hug. He felt just like she'd imagined. Strong and warm. Steady and—

"I hate to interrupt this sweet family moment," Charlotte said. "But shouldn't we get a move on?"

"You're right, Charlotte. We should leave soon," Ernest said. "They should be getting here any second."

"Actually . . . we might have a few more minutes," Director Harlow said. "The Nicks of Time might be a little preoccupied at the moment."

"Why do you say that?" Ernest asked.

"Well . . . after they transformed into a gigantic sand monster, we used a flamethrower on them and turned them into glass," Ray said.

Ernest stared at Cassandra with a look of total bewilderment.

"You killed them?" he said.

"No, we didn't kill them. Just slowed them down, I think," Director Harlow replied.

"Even if the Nicks of Time aren't coming after us, we should still be getting back soon," Charlotte said. "My parents are probably freaking out right about now."

Ernest shook his head. "No. I'm sorry, but we can't go back yet," he said.

"Whaaat?" Ray whined. "Why not?"

Ernest let out a hefty sigh. He shuffled his leather shoes against the ground.

"I left quite a few traces of myself out there in the timeline. And I'm sure you all did, too," Ernest said. "If we don't undo them now, the Cloak Folks—uh, I mean the Nicks of Time— will never stop chasing us. And the last thing I want is them following us back home to our present time."

"Are you saying what I think you're saying?" Charlotte said.

"Yes," he said. "We need to go back through all of those time coordinates and undo all the changes we've made."

"Are you serious right now?" Ray lamented. "But we just went through them all! Do we really have to go back? Why'd you leave so many traces?"

"Well, first, I quickly realized that the more traces I left scattered all over the timeline, the harder it was for the Cloak Folks to find me. It confused their senses, I think. They had a harder time tracking me down the more interfering I did with the timeline. And . . . I suppose, there was always a tiny part of me that held out hope for a moment like this," he said. "Hoping that maybe if I left enough clues, somebody could come find me."

"But you've been everywhere!" Charlotte said. "It'll take years to go back through the entire time loop!"

"I promise it won't take that long," Ernest said. "I've gotten pretty good at making quick time traveling pit stops over the last decade. And it's going to be so much easier with an actual time machine!"

He motioned toward the machine before jumping up with a start and catching Director Harlow's hand.

"Oh! I almost forgot," Ernest said. "I have something for you."

He swung the leather bag hanging from his back around toward his chest. He reached in and pulled out a small item that looked like it was wrapped in newspapers from the 1800s. Director Harlow unwrapped the gift and her jaw dropped.

"No. Don't tell me this is what I think it is." She turned it over in her hand. Viv could see it was a small glass beaker, engraved with two initials: MC.

MC? A beaker? No way. Is that Marie Curie's?

"Think we need to return this, too?" Ernest asked with a smile.

Viv's mom laughed as another round of tears fell down her cheeks. As the group stepped into the time machine, the sound of the hospital-room door made them all stop in their tracks. It was the nurse in the orange scrubs.

"Um, excuse me?!" the nurse said. "You all can't be in here! And what in the world is that thing?!"

"Guess that's our cue to exit stage right," Ernest said with a shrug.

The six of them piled into the time machine and shut the doors on the slack-jawed, stunned nurse.

"Gosh, it feels good to be back in this thing," Ernest said, working like a magician over the dashboard. "I never thought I'd get to see one again."

"You built this, right?" Viv asked, her eyes sparkling with wonder.

"Yep. That's right," he said. "There are parts of this machine that nobody else even knows about."

Ernest reached up toward the ceiling and flipped open a hidden metal panel, revealing a covert switch that read HYPERSPEED.

"*Hyperspeed?*" Ray said. "You're telling me we've been in slow mode this whole time?"

"Hold on," Ernest said with a smile.

Viv couldn't help but laugh, watching her embarrassed father smooth over the "EB" initials he'd carved into the recently constructed Great Wall of China.

In Ancient Greece, Ray cringed at all the naked athletes competing in the first ever Olympic Games, while Ernest returned one of the medals he'd earned after competing in the discus competition.

In the year 3652, during the invasion of the Brain Suckers, Ernest had to borrow a high-powered hose to clear off a rather large self-portrait painted on a mountainside, meant to confuse the alien invaders and give the surviving humans a chance to escape.

They bounced around from place to place as quickly as the time machine could carry them. One by one, every trace of the time traveling Ernest Becker disappeared from history. Cassandra and the kids' traces were next. After they made a few pit stops to clean up the vomit Ray had left behind, they set their coordinates for the present.

Back to Area 51.

Back home.

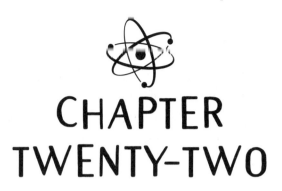

CHAPTER TWENTY-TWO

With the two adults and four kids squeezed in tight, the time machine had reached its maximum capacity. The doors opened and spat everyone out onto the floor of Area 51's Continuum Navigation wing, almost like the machine itself was exhausted and sick of having so many people inside of it.

"Oh, thank goodness!" Mr. Mond exclaimed.

"CHARLOTTE PATRICIA FRANK!" Charlotte's parents shouted in unison.

"Mijo!" Lieutenant Padilla cried.

All of the parents who had been waiting back at the base were crowded around the row of time machines. One by one, each retrieved their woozy child off the floor and wrapped them in relieved hugs.

"Is this real?" Viv said, rubbing at her tired eyes. "Did it work? Are we actually back?"

"How long were we gone?" Elijah said into his father's chest.

"About a millisecond," Dr. Frank said.

"A millisecond?!" Elijah said. "Are you kidding me?! It felt like we were gone for . . . well, forever!"

Mr. Mond lovingly brushed some of Ray's hair out of his eyes, before shaking the already motion-sick boy.

"You are SO grounded, young man," Mr. Mond said.

"But, Dad! I met da Vinci!" Ray said, his dizzy gaze spinning around the room.

"I don't care who you met!" Mr. Mond yelled. "Do you realize how much danger you put yourself in?!"

"You don't have to worry about that," Ray said, gripping at his stomach and turning even more green. "Trust me . . . I'm never time traveling ever again!" He tripped over his own feet, landed on his hands and knees, and released one final deluge of puke.

"Oh, come on! Don't pull a Ray all over the floor!" his dad complained. "Now I have to clean that up!"

"Hold on . . . What did you just say?" Ray asked, wiping a dribble from his chin. "Did you just say 'pull a Ray'?"

The parents who had remained at the base looked at one another like Ray was crazy.

"Yeah?" Mr. Frank said. "You know? Like to 'pull a Ray'? To throw up?"

"That's not a saying!" Ray said.

"Yes, it is," Dr. Frank chimed in.

"Nuh-uh!" Ray protested. "You're lying!"

"No, it's true. Look it up if you want!" Mr. Frank said.

In a flash, Ray whipped out the trusty iPhone 42 from his pocket and spoke into the end he thought was the receiver. "Hey, iPhone. Define 'pulling a Ray.'"

The automated voice of the phone's AI system was as clear as day. "'Pulling a Ray' is an American idiom originating from the 1970s. It translates to vomiting."

"What?! How the heck did that happen?" Ray said.

"You mean you guys don't know that saying?" Dr. Frank asked.

"Huh," Director Harlow said. "Something you kids did when you were out there in the timeline must've affected the evolution of the American English language."

"Oh, that's just great!" Ray said, throwing his arms up in the air. "Exactly the way I want to be immortalized!"

"Wait, so, Mr. Mond—that means that you named Ray after a slang word for puke?" Viv asked.

Mr. Mond gave a shrug of his shoulders. "What? It's a family name."

The last to step out of the time machine doors was the man of the hour: Ernest Becker. Viv watched as the shock she felt back in the hospital room washed over all the other parents.

"You've got to be kidding me," Charlotte's mom said. Both she and Desmond let go of their daughter, rising to their feet to get a better look at the man who might as well have been a living ghost.

". . . Ern?" Desmond said. "I can't believe it!"

"Ernest Becker! Back in Area 51!" Lieutenant Padilla said. "Well, I'll be a monkey's uncle!"

Ernest was welcomed back like a long-lost friend, each of his former coworkers meeting him with a warm embrace.

Dr. Frank whipped her head around to Director Harlow. "You did it? You actually found him?"

"I didn't do it by myself," Viv's mom said. "The kids helped, too. In fact, they saved my life. Yet again! I would've been a goner if it wasn't for your son, Al."

"Atta boy, Ray!" Mr. Mond said with glee.

"Speaking of which," Director Harlow continued, "Ray, what is that device you have?" Director Harlow asked.

"Oh, you mean this?" Ray said, holding up his shiny new device. "It's an iPhone 42! I got it from the future! Apparently, Joanna and I are going to invent this one day!"

"Joanna?" Director Harlow said skeptically. "You're saying that in the future, Joanna works here?"

Ray nodded.

"Hmm . . . Perhaps I should consider giving her a second chance . . . ," Director Harlow pondered aloud.

"Um, Ray? You brought that iPhone back to the present?" Viv said. "Weren't we supposed to leave everything? What if the Nicks of Time come after us here?"

"Whoops. I also brought this back," Elijah said, holding up the futuristic flight marble.

"This is technology from the future?" Dr. Frank said, examining the devices in the kids' hands.

"What do you think, Ernest?" Director Harlow said. "Should we return this stuff back to where they got it?"

"Let me see those for a second?" Ernest said, extending his hand. Charlotte, Elijah, and Ray forked over their gadgets. With a quick sidestep, Ernest got back into the time machine, spun the dial on his temporal transporter, closed the doors, and slammed down on the lever.

Viv didn't even have time to react. Nobody in the room did. A nanosecond later, the doors of the time machine reopened with a wheeze of vapor. Ernest stepped out and dusted off his hands.

"There! Back in 2050 where they belong. Now how about we stick around here for a little while?" Ernest said. "I'm hoping it'll be a long time before I step into one of those time machines again."

"What do you mean, Ern?" Desmond said. "Surely, you're going to come back to work here at the base, right?"

Ernest pursed his lips and scratched at the back of his head, seeming to consider the proposition. But it wasn't long before Viv could see the determination settle in on his face.

"I think I've had enough adventure for a lifetime. For fifty lifetimes!"

"So, you're just going to leave this all behind?" Lieutenant Padilla said, motioning to the bay of experimental time machines. "You're the greatest chronometrist the world has ever known! No one's ever been able to fill your shoes since you left. You invented time travel, for crying out loud!"

"I think it's time for the next generation to take over," he said, giving Viv another one of his patented winks. "Plus, 'stay-at-home' dad has a pretty nice ring to it."

"Really?" Viv said. "But you're a scientist!"

"The job of a scientist is to seek the answers to the questions that they care about. And right now, the only thing I care about is getting to know you," he said, pulling her in for another hug.

Viv hadn't thought it was possible to hug him any tighter, but she managed it. Hearing those words come from her dad was all she'd ever wanted.

"I can't wait to get to know you, either," Viv said. "I have about a billion questions."

"Whatever number of questions you have for me, I have double for you," he said. "I need to hear about every class, every homework assignment, every crush, everything."

Viv could feel her cheeks flush with embarrassment. It took everything in her power not to lock eyes with Elijah. She wasn't ready to make her feelings for him that obvious . . . *yet*. For the first time in her life, Viv realized that she'd never really had anyone to talk to about those kinds of things. No adult, at least. With her mom always at work, most days, she'd come home from school and be completely alone.

The thought of having a dad around . . . Not just any dad, but *her* dad, made the waterworks come rushing back. Ernest squeezed her tighter still. The warmth of his hug filled her with a sense of ease as she spoke the words she'd been waiting to say her entire life.

"I love you, Da—"

Before she could get out the final word, a sharp alarm shrieked through the hall.

Oh no. Please. Not now!

CHAPTER
TWENTY-THREE

"You have got to be kidding me," Ernest cried. "I just got home, and you're telling me that something's wrong again?"

Not wasting a moment, Director Harlow opened up the Central Brain and examined the report that had come in from another internal department. Her lined face looked even more worn out as she read.

"Well, that's not good," she said.

"What is it?" Mr. Frank asked.

"It's the core," Director Harlow said. "It stopped spinning."

". . . The core?" Charlotte asked. "The core of what?"

"The Earth," Director Harlow replied. "The molten iron core stopped spinning, which means the magnetic field that surrounds the planet has completely dissipated."

"You're right. That doesn't sound good," Ray said.

"What does that mean for us?" Viv asked.

"The lack of the protective magnetic field will slowly expose the Earth to a dangerous amount of solar particles from the sun. From these readouts, it looks like there are already a number of satellites in distress."

Viv felt two heavy hands lay gently down onto her shoulders. It was her dad, his chest heavy with a resigned sigh.

"This must've been something I did," Ernest said.

"No, no! Don't be so hard on yourself, Ernest," Desmond said. "We don't know what caused this. It could've been anything."

Ernest raised a skeptical eyebrow.

"I've been traveling through time for over a decade. The second I return home, suddenly the Earth's core stops spinning? No. This can't be a coincidence."

There was a long stretch of quiet in the room. The silence was only broken when Viv spoke up.

"He's right," she said in support. "Who knows what kind of havoc we might've accidentally caused. In all of those different eras? There's gotta be something one of us did while we were out there. And with the Nicks still stuck as glass, there's no one to keep the peace in the timeline."

It was quiet for a moment as the realization sunk in.

Wow. Who would've thought that a girl just trying to get her dad back could stop the rotation of the Earth's core?

"What's our best option?" Desmond said.

Director Harlow considered it for a moment before snapping her fingers.

"We could try a targeted electromagnetic pulse. If it's

strong enough, it could get the atomic poles back into alignment. Kind of like shocking a heart back to life."

There was a knock at the door. A woman with her hair cropped short entered in a huff.

"Director Harlow? Ma'am?" the woman said, "The Earth's magnetic field—"

"Has collapsed. Yes, I just read the report. Any word from the White House?" Cassandra said.

The woman tapped her heels together and stood at attention.

"Yes, ma'am. I just got off the phone with the president," the woman said. "They're calling for Operation TerraMarathon."

Cassandra shook her head and clicked her tongue against the roof of her mouth.

"Already?" she said. "Guess I'd rather them act too fast than too slow."

"What in the heck is Operation TerraMarathon?" Charlotte said.

"It's exactly what it sounds like," Director Harlow replied. "It's a race to the center of the Earth."

Viv's eyes widened at the prospect.

No way. No freaking way.

"Are you saying what I think you're saying?" she asked.

"That's right. We'll need to go down there. And it sounds like we won't be the only ones. Area 51 is not the only covert scientific base," Cassandra explained. "Many countries all around the world have their own hidden high-level research labs."

"And everyone will be racing to get to the core first," Dr. Frank added.

"Why?" Viv said.

"Because who doesn't want to be the country that saves the world?" Director Harlow said with a smile.

"Director Harlow!" Ernest said, standing over the Central Brain. "Looks like the United Kingdom just launched their drill."

"Well, then it sounds like we better get going," Director Harlow said. "I've heard the Brits are fast. They'll be down there drinking a cup of tea if we don't leave soon. Kids? You guys wanna come?"

"I do!" Elijah said.

"Me too!" Charlotte chimed in.

"Why not?" Ray said.

"Viv?" her mom asked.

Viv couldn't hide the smile that was spreading across her face. Her mom actually wanted her help and wasn't trying to misguidedly protect her. She trusted Viv. After everything they'd been through in the last week, Viv knew they still had a ways to go before things were back to normal between them. But they'd get there; she knew they would.

A huge yawn escaped from her mouth before she got out

her response. All of the action, using her powers, and the emotions of seeing her dad were finally catching up to her.

"You can sleep on the way down," Cassandra promised. "It's about eighteen hundred miles until we reach the core. It'll take a few hours before we get there."

"Eighteen hundred miles?!"

"Will we be okay?" Ray said. "I've heard it gets pretty hot down there."

"Oh, we'll be more than fine," Director Harlow said. "Just wait until you see our ride."

Viv looked to Ernest for his input. He raised a knowing eyebrow. It was like telepathy. She could almost read his mind, hearing him urge her to indulge in her adventurous side.

Go. You only live once.

"Okay, I'm in."

"Then I'm coming, too," her dad quickly followed up.

"Really? You're sure you don't want to stay here and rest, Ern?" Cassandra said. "We can get you a spot in the infirmary. The doctors should probably check you out. You look a little skinny."

"And bald," Mr. Mond pointed out.

"Not sure the infirmary can help with that last part," Ernest said with a rub of his head.

"You'd be surprised," Ray said. "I heard they have spray-on hair in a can!"

"No, I think the best thing for me is to be with family right now," Ernest said, slinging an arm around Director Harlow's and Viv's shoulders. "I'm not leaving you two ever again."

He leaned over and planted a big fat kiss on Cassandra's lips.

Gross. Guess I didn't anticipate that I'd have to see that *for the rest of my life.*

"Okay, enough kissing, you two," Viv said. "We've got a planet to save."

ACKNOWLEDGMENTS

JAMES S. MURRAY

First and foremost, a huge thanks to my amazingly talented writing partner Carsen Smith, without whom this book series would not be possible.

Thanks to our fantastic colleagues at Penguin—Rob Valois, Francesco Sedita, Alex Wolfe, Lizzie Goodell, and the entire team that brought Area 51 to life.

Thanks to my colleagues Joseph, Nicole, and Ethan. Thanks to Jack Rovner and Dexter Scott from Vector Management; Brandi Bowles from UTA; Danny Passman from GTRB; Phil Sarna, Mitch Pearlstein, and Cristian Hitchcock from PSBM; and Elena Stokes and the excellent team from Wunderkind PR. And special thanks to Brad Meltzer and R. L. Stine.

And most importantly, thanks to the most supportive, loving, creative person I know—my incredible wife, Melyssa.

Finally, thanks to all the young *Impractical Jokers* fans around the world. Remember—time is all we have, so don't waste time trying to chase it. Enjoy the present!

CARSEN SMITH

What started as a fun "what-if" conversation has since sprouted into a full-fledged world of supernatural creatures, gadgets, adventure, and now time travel. So, to James, thank you for being a true creative force and a brilliant writing partner.

To my beloved family and to all the friends who let me use their names as characters, I'd include you here, but you're already in the books, which seems like a pretty fair trade.

A heartfelt thank-you to our wonderfully supportive team at Penguin Random House—Alex Wolfe, Rob Valois, Francesco Sedita, Lizzie Goodell, and everyone else who helped make this series a reality. Thank you to Brandi Bowles at UTA and our team at Vector Management. To Joe T, Nicole, and Ethan for being extraordinary. And to the magnificent Elena Stokes at Wunderkind PR. None of it would be possible without your dedication and support.

To Will, for being an endless source of joy and laughter in my life. And to our cats, Goose and Buffy, for stepping on my laptop every time I tried to write.

And to anyone who finds themselves with a copy of Area 51 Interns, we hope you have as much fun reading it as we did writing it.

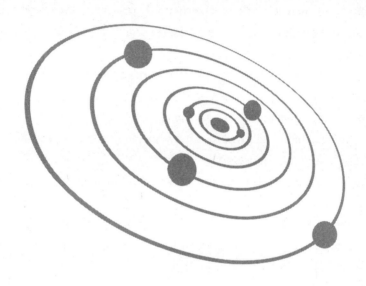